RICH TOWN POOR TOWN

Ghosts of Copper's Past

RICH TOWN POOR TOWN

Ghosts of Copper's Past

Roberto Rabago

The Awakened Press

The Awakened Press
www.theawakenedpress.com

For information about special discounts or for bulk purchases, please contact
The Awakened Press at books@theawakenedpress.com.

PRINTING HISTORY
MultiCultural Educational Publishing Company
Jamie Moffett
First Printing September 2011
Second Printing December 2011
Third Printing October 2012

Published in 2011 by Copper Star Publishing LLC

Front Cover Photo: The ruins of the family home of the author, Jerome, AZ. Photo © Bob Swanson of Swanson Images.
Back Cover Photo: Courtesy of Arizona State Parks. Photo is displayed in the Jerome Historic State Park.
Author Photo: Jeanette Gibler
Original Cover Design: Jamie Moffett

2024 Cover Design: Kurt A. Dierking II
2024 Book Editor: Lindsay R.A. Dierking

Printed in the United States of America

ISBN: 979-8-9912770-4-4

Dedicated—

True to my heritage, I dedicate this work to my mother, Concepción Yañez Rábago, who held our family together with her love, even in the most difficult of times and circumstances.

I also wish to dedicate this to a special teacher, Miss Fay Ivey. After writing these stories and reflecting on growing up in Jerome, I realized how much she changed the direction of my life.

The Little Daisy Mine, Jerome, Arizona. Courtesy of The Jerome Historical Society.

CONTENTS

ACKNOWLEDGMENTS

There are many people to whom I owe thanks, but unfortunately, I can only specify a few. To those I do not name, I hope that you will take note of how each of you have contributed, and accept my gratitude.

I thank my wife, children and sister for urging me along. I thank Mairi Ross and Jamie Moffett of MCE Publishing. Had it not been for Mairi's perceptiveness and encouragement in the beginning, I may have never made the effort required to write. After the stories were written, I realized how many thanks I owe to Jim Byrkit, for his trail blazing work, Forging the Copper Collar.

I give grateful acknowledgment to:

The Jerome Historical Society, Jerome, Arizona, for the photo of the U. V. Smelter, the Little Daisy Mine, and the copy of the 1899 Jerome Ordinance.

Sharlott Hall Museum, Prescott, Arizona, for permission to reprint "Juan of the Slag Pots," by Sharlot Hall.

Phoenix Art Museum, for permission to reprint the works of Lew Davis: Little Boy Lives in a Copper Camp, and Morning at the Little Daisy. Mr. Davis lived and worked in Jerome for many years.

Henry Holt and Company, LLC, for "Here Dead Lie We Because We Did Not Choose," from The Collected Poems of A. E. Housman, copyright 1924,1965, by Henry Holt and Company. Reprinted by permission of Henry Holt and Company LLC.

Arizona State Parks, for permission to reprint the photograph of two miners working underground, one of whom is my father. The photo is displayed in the Jerome Historic State Park.

History of Jerome, by Lewis J. MacDonald, unpublished master's thesis, Jerome Public Library.

Bob Swanson of Swanson Images (swansonimages. com) for the cover photo of the ruins of my childhood home in Jerome.

Beachesonlocation.com, Cottonwood, Arizona, for the author's photograph.

Although I gratefully acknowledge all of those who helped make this book possible, all of the facts as presented in this book, and of course all of the opinions and conclusions, are my sole responsibility.

Morning at the Little Daisy by Lew Davis.
Courtesy of the Phoenix Art Museum.

Author's Preface

"I wonder what living in Jerome was like when this was a mining town? What kind of lives did the miners live? What other kinds of people lived here? Did they have a good life? Were they happy, or was their life very hard?" Questions like these are often asked by many present-day visitors to Jerome.

These short stories have been written to answer some of those questions. I feel qualified to answer them because I was born in Jerome, and raised in Jerome. In fact, I grew up in the house pictured on the cover of this book. I was the son of a miner.

I graduated from Jerome High School, then left to live in California for a good while. However, I always returned to Jerome year after year, if only for a few days at a time. In my lifetime, I have seen Jerome as a living, working mining town, saw it die, then saw it weakly returned to life by hippies and artists, until it revived and became the thriving "ghost town" that it is today. I can say that I have lived a good part of my life here in Jerome.

These stories are not imaginary; I have lived through most of them. The core elements of all these stories are true. Of course, some parts of the stories have been dramatized and fictionalized, but only to present the basic truths in a readable and entertaining way. I have kept them as factual and honest as possible.

Keep in mind that the world of Jerome a century ago was a completely different world than today's world. Then, there were no labor unions, no Fair Labor Standards Act, no OSHA, no anti-discrimination laws, no welfare, no worker's compensation, no minimum wage, no unemployment insurance, on and on. Neither did a world of independent law and justice exist, because the all-powerful mining companies were not restrained in any way by the regulations and laws that did exist. The mining companies were the law.

When I started to write these stories, I did not have any particular point of view to advance. I had no initial intent to praise or criticize Jerome. My object was to give the reader an idea of what it was like to have been born and to have grown up in Jerome. I thought that the best way to accomplish this was to write about different incidents that had occurred in my life, incidents that made an impression on me. I believe that these stories do accurately convey an idea of what Jerome was like during its life as a mining town.

These stories are written from an entirely different perspective than most other books that have been written about Jerome. They are written from the perspective of a person who grew up in Jerome, poor, in a miner's family, and a member of a dominated minority. From this perspective, growing up in Jerome was both wonderful and brutal.

Other books about Jerome cover very well the lives of the powerful men who created Jerome: men like William A. Clark, men of the Douglas family, and others. You may perhaps notice that I said these men were "powerful," but did not say that these men were "great," which is the way that they are more commonly described. I do not deny that these men were both bold and brave, for they gambled huge fortunes on a grand scale. They took immense risks in investing huge amounts of capital to build railroads and smelters in this lonely place, on the expectation that they could successfully "exploit" the ore bodies that they hoped and expected to find.

It is ironic that the term "exploit" has a double meaning when applied to mining. In mining terms, to "exploit" means to develop a mine, to make it a successful and profitable venture. But the word "exploit," in the more general sense, means to take advantage of a person or a situation in an unfair or unethical manner. These stories tell of life in Jerome that was quite brutal, so "exploitation," in the sense of making use of people unfairly or unethically, is the sense that is applied in them.

Please don't misunderstand me. I love Jerome, and have always loved it, especially when I was growing up here. But after composing these stories and reviewing them as a whole, I realized that the picture of Jerome that I had painted was not a pretty one. From my stories emerged a picture of Jerome, that in my maturity, I could recognize as a penal or colonial colony. That realization was a shock to me, because when I started writing I had no pre-conceived notion of Jerome as anything other than a great place to live.

The term penal colony usually refers to a place where convicted criminals or other undesirables are forced to perform hard labor by guards armed with whips or guns. They are confined to their work-site by guards with weapons or by physical surroundings. The salt mines of Sardinia or Devil's Island in French

Guiana come to mind.

Comparing Jerome to a penal colony is not an exact analogy, because the miners of Jerome were not convicted criminals who were sentenced to live in Jerome; they chose to live here voluntarily. But Jerome was a place very difficult to get to, and it was also a very difficult place to leave, so the element of coercion by the surroundings was certainly present.

I admit that a more exact analogy is to compare Jerome to a colonial outpost. A colonial outpost differs from a penal colony in that the laborers in a colonial outpost are not sentenced convicts; they are free men working voluntarily. Rather than working under an overt threat of force or arms, they are forced to work because of economic need. They work in order to survive, but they have no control of their pay or their working conditions; the employer has all the power. The workers are only replaceable, interchangeable parts, like parts of a machine.

However, both penal colonies and colonial outposts have in common harsh working conditions. Both are operated for the benefit of absentee owners who receive the wealth far away, in much more comfortable surroundings.

My insight into Jerome as a penal colony began when I became aware of an ancient copper mine near the Dead Sea, in Jordan. In 2002, an archaeological excavation found the remains of a very large copper mining and smelting operation carbon-dated to the tenth century before Christ, almost 3000 years ago. The place is called Khirbat en Nahas, which means "remains of copper" in Arabic. The site contains a large slag dump, the residue from the mining and smelting of copper. The size of the slag dump indicates that the site was a large operation, one that would require a large number of people to live and work nearby.

The mine was located in a hot, dry desert without water or shelter; it was not the type of place that people would freely choose to settle. It was not close to any cities or settlements. Remains of stone guardhouses are found around the site, so it can be inferred that the people who labored at the mine and smelter were coerced by armed guards to live and work and die there. A few miles from the mines, there is a large cemetery that contains 3500 tombs.

Upon learning of this excavation, I was struck by the similarity of copper mining thirty centuries ago in Khirbat en Nahas to copper mining in Jerome, Arizona, one century ago.

"What?" a reader might ask. "Are you suggesting that this quaint, charming, historic, arty, touristy place that is Jerome today was like an ancient slave labor camp?" Yes I am.

Aside from the fact that both Jerome and Khirbat en Nahas were copper mining camps, let me raise some other similarities. First, there is a similarity in the remoteness of locations. Khirbat en Nahas was not on any trading route; it was an out-of-the-way place. Jerome also was located away from the few population centers in Arizona. In the early days, there were no roads into Jerome, only trails. The climate of Jerome was inhospitable, especially in winter. There was no water in Jerome; the nearest springs were miles away. Even the Native Americans that populated the Verde Valley did not live in Jerome.

The remoteness of Jerome, isolated in the mountains, with no easy transportation, was a hard obstacle to overcome for miners who lived from paycheck to paycheck. They had to walk to get to Jerome. If they did not like the life after they got here, there was no place else to work, because all the mine owners of Arizona worked in concert. A person fired from Jerome would not be able to find employment in any other mine in Arizona. For this reason, many miners put up with the hard life in Jerome, because they really had little choice. The coercion of the surroundings was present.

Jerome had another feature of a penal colony or colonial outpost, which was also present at Khirbat en Nahas: the persons who benefited from the labor did not live at the work sites. At Khirbat en Nahas, the beneficiaries were probably rulers who lived in comfort in Egypt, far from the desert. In Jerome, the beneficiaries were dwellers in the Eastern financial centers where they lived in much more comfortable surroundings.

But there are still other similarities which compare Jerome to Khirbat en Nahas. Consider the matter of the tombs. At Khirbat en Nahas there were 3500 tombs located near the mine. Since there were no large population centers nearby, it is reasonable to assume that the bodies all came from deaths that occurred at the mine. In Jerome, there are no comparable huge cemeteries. However, Jerome had six large hospitals (not all operating at the same time). Injury and death in the mines was common. In Jerome, most of the medical records were intentionally destroyed. Entire cemeteries are not well-documented, much less individual graves. It is therefore impossible at this time to know the number of the deaths in the Jerome mines.

Consider also the matter of armed guards. At Khirbat en Nahas, the ancient location, the presence of armed guards is inferred from the stone guard houses that ringed the mine. In Jerome, the means of subjugation was not as overt as that. The miners were controlled by economics. This economic subjugation was effective enough when the wages were set at the bare subsistence level. The mine owners were capable of shutting down the mines for six months in order to break a worker's strike that called for an increase in wages of 25 cents a day—a raise of 2 cents an hour. No miner's family could survive without wages for six months.

But if more direct action was needed, the guns came out. In the Jerome Deportation of 1917, more than a hundred miners were shipped in cattle cars, at gunpoint, to the border with California, and dumped there. The following day, more than a thousand miners were shipped in cattle cars, at gunpoint, from Bisbee, Arizona, and dumped in the middle of the desert in New Mexico. Communications between the mine owners of Jerome and Bisbee are indicative that there was close coordination in both deportations, and suggest that the Jerome Deportation was a "dress rehearsal" for the Bisbee Deportation.

The deportees were all characterized, of course, as "outside agitators," or "trouble-makers." In fact, nearly all the deportees were simply men that the mining companies wanted to be rid of, because they objected to their poor pay or dangerous working conditions, and wanted to organize for better bargaining power with the mine owners.

There is even a darker side to the deportations. It is not so well known that the mine owners planted their own hired goons to incite the incidents in the mines. These incidents were subsequently used to justify their armed interventions. In this way, they got rid of any workers who did not meekly submit to them. No, there was no ring of armed guards surrounding Jerome, but the armed might was always present, hidden out of sight, but always ready for use.

These similarities between Jerome and Khirbat en Nahas are the "ghosts" that are referred to in the title of this book. These ghosts still haunt Jerome, and Arizona, today.

For readers who want to learn more about life in a mining town in Arizona, I strongly recommend the book, *Forging the Copper Collar,* by Jim Byrkit. Professor Byrkit documents the history of labor relations in Arizona. I also strongly recommend *The Great Arizona Orphan Abduction,* by Linda Gordon. Ms. Gordon carefully documents an incident that happened in the Clifton-Morenci mining camp of Arizona in 1903. The social and labor relations that she describes as existing in Clifton-Morenci are exactly those that existed in Jerome for the next half century that followed.

It is my hope that Arizona will leave the more brutal aspects of its history behind and become a place where people of all economic backgrounds, races, ethnicities, and skin color will have an equal opportunity to contribute their part to this state.

U. V. Smelter, Jerome, Arizona. Courtesy of The Jerome Historical Society.

Juan of the Slag Pots

Soon-to-be-doctor Anthony J. Murrieta let his mind wander from the words of President Gilman of the University of California. At the conclusion of the president's speech, he would be awarded his Medical Doctor degree. He silently played with the words: Doctor Murrieta, Doctor A. J. Murrieta, Doctor Anthony J. Murrieta, placing the emphasis on doctor. Finally, he would be able to put the skills he had learned to good purposes. He would no longer have to stand by helplessly when people suffered and died from lack of medical care, much less good, caring medical care.

His eyes wandered from the speaker's stand to the sight of San Francisco Bay. The warmth of the sun in May had dissipated the morning fog of the Berkeley hills, but there was still a mist low over the waters of the bay. The white wakes of the ferry boats converging on the Ferry Building were the first to catch his eye. He tried to focus past the Ferry Building to the hospital where he had done his surgical training. Near it was the apartment where he had lived for the past four years, a small, furnished apartment that did not get much sun except when the afternoon sun reflected off the building across the street.

He thought of the great earthquake and fire that had leveled and ravaged much of the city only seven years earlier. He wished that he had been a trained doctor at that time so that he could have made life easier for the injured.

Murrieta's mind was brought back to the ceremony when he noticed that classmates near him were fidgeting and staring at the back of his chair. Then he realized that the back legs were sinking very slowly down into the moist grass, and that he would topple over backwards if the sinking continued. He took care of the problem by edging forward on his chair, and supported more of his weight on his own legs.

He then turned his attention to President Gilman, who was just concluding his speech. "I urge you future doctors to become more than dispensers of medicine and experts in diseases, but rather to become students of life in the larger scope of its relations."

My feelings exactly, thought Murrieta, although he had never put them so clearly in words. President Gilman concluded with the words of the Hippocratic Oath. "Above all, do no harm to anyone."

"Of course," thought soon-to-be-doctor Murrieta. "How else could a good doctor act?"

The doctor-candidates applauded the end of the speech with a round of applause that was reserved, in keeping with their new dignity, and one by one they crossed the podium to receive their diplomas. As Murrieta extended his hand to receive his diploma, the president said, "Come to my office next Monday at nine o'clock. I have received something that you may be interested in."

At 8:55 am the following Monday, Doctor Murrieta was at the president's office, although he did not knock on the door until nine o'clock sharp, in order not to appear too eager. He approached the president's desk as if to sit on one of the chairs in front of the desk where the students always sat, but President Gilman had moved from around his desk, and motioned Doctor Murrieta to the leather chairs where he received peers and honored guests. He had a letter in his hand.

He said, "Tell me what you think of this offer. It is a request for a surgeon from a mining company in Arizona, in a place called Jerome. They have a new fifty-bed hospital, they provide living quarters, plenty of patients to keep you busy, and a handsome salary. Are you interested?"

"Certainly. Did they ask for anything else other than a surgeon?"

"They wanted most of all a good surgeon, one with some experience in treating trauma. I know you're a good surgeon, and you have had trauma experience. They also wanted someone who was rugged enough for a mining town." President Gilman looked over the top of his glasses to look again at Doctor Murrieta. He saw a man a good four inches taller than the other men in his class, with bigger hands and broader shoulders than most surgeons. The heavy eyebrows gave his face something of a fierce look that indicated a man who could take care of himself if he needed to.

"I told them that you had grown up in the gold-mining part of the state, and they asked if you were related to the bandit Joaquin Murrieta. They also asked if you were Spanish or Mexican."

"You are right, sir. I grew up in Sonora, California, so I know life in mining towns. Murrieta is a very common name in those parts."

He also said, "I am Spanish," because he knew

that more doors would be open to him that way.

"Well, they gave me full authority to choose the man for them. I think you are good enough and rugged enough for them. You are my choice for the job, so the job is yours, if you want it."

One week later, Doctor Murrieta was on a train, on his way to Jerome, Arizona. He left San Francisco on the Southern Pacific Railway and transferred to the Santa Fe Railroad in Los Angeles, heading eastward. He marveled at the beauty of San Bernardino, with its miles of green orange groves and mountains topped with snow. He hoped Arizona would be half as beautiful.

"Maybe Jerome will not be too bad," he thought.

After two days, the train arrived at Ash Fork, Arizona, where he transferred to the Prescott-Phoenix line, and got off at Jerome Junction. He did not see anything that looked like a town, and there was no mine to be seen. He was told that this junction was merely a transfer point between the main line and a narrow gauge railway that would take him to Jerome itself.

The train to Jerome was comprised of a string of cars open at the top that were used to haul mining equipment, the one passenger coach that he was riding in, and an elegantly appointed private railroad coach.

"That car belongs to Mr. Clarkston, who owns all of Jerome," someone said.

The train left Jerome Junction and followed a gradually climbing route across a high-desert valley made green by scrub juniper trees. The train skirted around a large mountain on the right, then the road turned southwards on the east side of the mountain. Doctor Murrieta looked out the windows on the left-hand side, and saw a valley about fifty miles wide, covered with green trees that followed a winding river, and green grasses covering the rest.

But the remarkable part was the eastern horizon that was formed not by the curve of the earth meeting the sky, but rather by a ridge of mountains flat across the top, that extended from the north to the south. More remarkable, the ridges had a natural valance of rocks 1000-feet high that reflected different shades of color, from bright red, to pink, to blue, to white. The colors changed as the train moved, and with the passage of the sun.

"I have never seen a natural scene as beautiful as this. Maybe Jerome itself will be beautiful also," he told himself.

"Jerome Station up ahead. End of the line!"

The phrase "end of the line" was echoing in his mind as the train came to a stop, and Doctor Murrieta stepped out of the train onto the concrete platform. The words in his mind were lost in the whanking, clanging, rasping, ratcheting, clinking, whistling, hissing sounds of what seemed to be a steel mill in full operation.

He had heard stamping mills back in the California gold country, but this was more like a hundred stamping mills all going at the same time. The air smelled of sulfur, like rotten eggs, that hurt his lungs when he breathed. This was the end of the line. The train had stopped in the middle of this steel monster that would have seemed more appropriate in the steel towns of Ohio, but was totally unexpected and out of place on this barren mountain.

Doctor Murrieta saw workmen going about their business, moving from one building to another. Their clothing was made of coarse denim that once may have been blue, but was now covered with a dull gray dust that settled on their clothes, and their faces. Their spirits must also have been covered with the same dust, for their movements were mechanical and without enthusiasm.

"I wonder if this is what hell looks like?" he thought as his heart sank.

At that moment, Doctor Murrieta felt a hand on his shoulder and heard a man's voice say, "Welcome to Jerome!"

The doctor turned around to see a man dressed in a blue suit, with one hand extended in a handshake, and the other hand brushing the gray dust off his suit. He wore round spectacles with a gold frame. The man's voice was friendly when he said, "I'm Bill Clarkston," but his eyes did not match the friendliness in his voice.

Before he could compose himself, Doctor Murrieta, very unprofessionally, blurted out, "What the hell is this thing?"

"Why, this is our copper smelter! Isn't she a beauty? There is nothing like her in all of Arizona, not even at the Copper Queen in Bisbee! I'll be glad to give you a tour of the whole operation, when you're ready for it."

"I expected to see a small mining operation like the ones where I grew up, but this is huge!"

Mr. Clarkston smiled proudly. "Take your time. Whenever you're ready, just call me and I will be glad to show you around. Now, I'll take you to your new home so that you can rest from your long trip. Your house is down the hill, too far to walk, so we'll go in my wagon."

They started down a dirt road so steep that the horses were not pulling the wagon, but were holding it back. After they were away from the noise where normal conversation was easier, just to make small talk, Doctor Murrieta said, "I saw your railroad car back at Jerome Junction."

Mr. Clarkston said, "Oh, that isn't my car. It belongs to the owner and general manager, who is also named Clarkston. I am the assistant manager, among other things." By the way he said it, Doctor Murrieta knew that his host liked to be confused with the other Mr. Clarkston.

As they proceeded downhill, Doctor Murrieta looked back at the smelter, and saw a wide black band extending below it. "What causes that black earth?"

"That is our slag dump. After we smelt the copper, there is a part left over that is called slag. We dump it down the hill. You will know all about it, after I give you the tour."

Proceeding downhill, they passed a saloon made of light-red colored stone, then a Presbyterian Church. From there, Doctor Murrieta could see a group of half a dozen substantial buildings that formed the downtown of Jerome. They turned right and passed a couple of two-story stucco homes with cement steps leading up to them from the street. The Doctor was glad to think that one of these might be reserved for him, so he asked, "Which one of these two is mine?"

"Neither," said, Mr. Clarkston. "The first one belongs to the casket supplier, and the other to the undertaker. Your house is the next house past this garden, next to our hospital. It is the house that we provide for our surgeon. We're pretty proud of it."

The house that Mr. Clarkston pointed out was also two stories high, but was not like the boxy stucco of the first two. The elegant surgeon's house was designed by an architect who had obviously given it much thought, for it had French doors, arched windows, a red tile roof, and could have passed easily for an Italian villa. There was a small cottage at the corner of the house that was nearest to the hospital.

"That little house is for the gardener. Mrs. Johnson has her quarters upstairs, and she will be your maid and your cook. You can see that you will live next door to our hospital, but I think that you will find this arrangement very convenient."

The house was more than Doctor Murrieta had ever expected to live in, not even at the end of his medical career. He thought of his confining apartment in San Francisco in contrast to his new home, and thought to himself, "Maybe Jerome will turn out to be a good place, after all!"

The doctor's expression must have shown his pleasure, for Mr. Clarkston said, "We thought you would like it. You can see how much we value our surgeon. Get settled in. Mrs. Johnson will help you. I will drop by tomorrow to show you the hospital and introduce you to the staff."

Doctor Murrieta found that the quality of the hospital was as far beyond his expectations as his house had been, and the staff was competent. After several weeks, Doctor Murrieta had settled into a routine that did not tax his skills. Most days were spent repairing broken bones and smashed fingers, stitching up some nasty cuts, and caring for several cases of massive burns, accompanied by smoke inhalation. Doctor Murrieta told Mr. Clarkston that they needed a separate burn unit in the hospital, and Mr. Clarkston agreed.

The head nurse, who seemed to know everything that happened in town, told him that the burns and inhalation injuries were caused by a fire in the mine that had been burning for years. The fire had started when high-sulfide ores had been exposed to oxygen. He told her that he hoped he would be able to visit the underground workings to see for himself, although he could imagine the hellish working conditions in an atmosphere of poisonous sulfur gas, in temperatures high enough to cause the dehydration he had seen in his patients.

His first call at night to the hospital was a bad one. A miner had been brought into the hospital by his foreman. He was unconscious, with a broken arm and a badly mangled foot.

The foreman explained how the accident happened. He told Doctor Murrieta that the elevator cage bringing the man up was open except for a "safety" rail about waist high, but that there was only two inches of clearance between the cage and the vertical shaft. The cage jerked coming up, and a load of steel shifted and forced the miner's foot beyond the edge of the cage. The first cross-timber sheared off the steel safety cap of the shoe, and the next timber took off the toes. As the cage crawled to the top, each cross-timber took off a portion of the foot back to the ankle, so that the lower leg was a mangled mess of bones, tendons, nerves, blood, and wood chips.

The amputation was done expertly, and the patient was stabilized.

The hot summer weather turned to the cool sunny days of autumn. Finally, Doctor Murrieta's patient load was such that he could spare part of one day to tour the smelter. He would also have liked a tour of the underground tunnels, especially the sulfide ore areas, but by now he was already familiar enough with the operation of the mine to know that the Company would not allow him to risk an injury to himself.

As expected, Mr. Clarkston refused an underground visit, but he did arrange for the tour of the smelter that same afternoon. "Just don't wear one of your white lab coats," Mr. Clarkston advised.

Mr. Clarkston did agree to show the doctor all the surface operations, starting at the shafts where the ore came up in big buckets called "skips." The air coming up the shaft smelled like the now familiar rotten eggs. Then he was taken to the crusher, where three big rotating cylinders lifted the ore-bearing rocks up one side, and let them come crashing down onto other rocks. They followed the conveyor belts to the long, high building that housed the three blast furnaces

The furnaces were huge steel cylinders, almost two stories high. The building housing the furnaces had slanted open windows near the roof, to let out the heat, the soot, and the smell of the furnaces.

Mr. Clarkston asked, "Do you know what a blast furnace is, and how it works?"

"No, never in my life have I seen anything like this. I certainly did not expect to see one out here in the desert."

"Let me give you a quick explanation. The inside of these tanks is heated to 2300 degrees Fahrenheit, to melt the ore, and extract the copper. The temperature must be controlled carefully; if not, it could cause what is called a 'runaway furnace,' and that can cause a lot of other things to go wrong. Temperatures that high are above the melting point of most metals, so the tanks have to be lined inside with a special clay, otherwise the tanks themselves would melt.

"The ore is first broken up and crushed by those big noisy drums that you saw outside, and then is fed into the top of each furnace by a conveyor belt, as you can see up there. In the bottom of the furnace we burn coke, that is coal crushed into a real fine powder. Incidentally, the coke is brought here all the way from Wales. As the ore melts, it filters down by gravity, where it meets the gases produced by the burning coke. That causes a chemical reaction to precipitate copper of a good purity that settles into the bottom part of the furnace. Above the bottom layer of copper, there is formed another distinct layer that contains most of the impurities. That part is called slag, and it is worthless. The slag is drawn out the left side of the furnace into specially lined cars that take it outside for dumping down the hillside below the smelter."

Mr. Clarkston continued, "The slag looks like hot lava when it is first poured out, then it cools into the black residue that you noted when you first arrived in Jerome. That is the job of the man you see standing by the center furnace. That same man also draws out the molten copper from the right hand side of the furnace, which is poured into those molds that you see lined up on that side. Each mold produces an ingot of copper that weighs about four hundred pounds. The purpose of this entire operation is to produce that ingot of copper. Well, doctor, that is a very brief explanation, but if you would like, I can give you a more detailed explanation, complete with chemical reaction formulas."

"Thank you, Mr. Clarkston. Your explanation was quite sufficient. But I am wondering what the valves are made of, the valves that control the flow of copper and slag out of the furnace? Wouldn't they melt also?"

"I compliment your quick grasp of things, Doctor. You have identified the weakest part of this system. No metal valves exist which could withstand the temperatures, so we have to 'tap,' that is, 'punch out,' a hole in the clay that lines the tanks in order to extract the slag and copper. After the furnace is drained, we replace the clay in the tapped hole, and start the process over again. Most of the time, the system works very well, but occasionally we get a runaway furnace that can be very dangerous." Mr. Clarkston paused for a moment in deep thought before he continued. "That was a very good question. Do you have any others?"

Doctor Murrieta was slow in answering, because he was turning over in his mind the potential for a very serious accident with these furnaces. "No wonder this company needs a large hospital and good medical people!" he thought to himself. But he only replied, "Thank you for the tour. It was very interesting and enlightening, but I must get back to the hospital. Thanks, again."

It did not take long for the next serious accident to happen. A man was brought in with third degree burns on both hands and his right arm. Parts of both legs had been burned. The right leg was the worst with burns reaching halfway up the thigh. The skin, muscles and tendons were gone so that the tibula and fibula were visible. He was taken directly to the operating room.

The smell of burned flesh was the strongest smell in the room that usually smelled of alcohol, ether and antiseptic solutions. The only question in Doctor Murrieta's mind was where exactly to make the amputations. Certainly he wanted to save as much of the man's limbs as possible, but he had to take off enough to minimize infection and gangrene. There was no way to know in advance the proper choice, so he proceeded quickly and efficiently, using his best judgment.

He checked on his patient early the next morning, but the man was unconscious. Doctor Murrieta thought he recognized the patient as the man who was standing near the furnace during the tour. On the following day, the man was able to talk, although he was very heavily sedated.

"I am sorry that I had to amputate both legs, but there was no other way if I was to save your life."

The man responded in very broken English, but they managed to understand each other. "I don't blame you at all, doctor. You saved my life and I am most grateful."

"Are you Juan de la Cruz?" asked Doctor Murrieta, after he had looked at the patient's chart.

The man answered, "At your service," before he

lapsed into unconsciousness.

Doctor Murrieta treated Juan every day, but it was not until a week later that they were able to converse about the accident.

Juan said, "I had finished dumping the slag from furnace number three. Then I went to furnace number one to draw out the copper. I have done this for two years now, without any problems. My foreman was standing next to me and also my friend, Walter. George and Henry were standing close, waiting to get the copper into the molds. I waited until my foreman gave the order to tap, and when he gave the order, I punched into the clay with a long steel bar that I use. This time I don't know what happened. I heard a roar, then I fell backward from the heat and the flash of light. Everything happened so fast, but for some time, I don't know for how long, I didn't realize what had happened.

"I didn't see the foreman and the other men, but I saw Walter on his back and I think he was unconscious or so scared that he couldn't move. The furnace was spitting and sparking, and a tongue of molten fire, of molten copper was heading right towards Walter. I got up and put both arms under him. I tried to lift him with just my arms, but he was too heavy. I dropped down on one knee and was able to lift him out of the way. Then I felt the copper burn my feet and catch my pants on fire. The next thing I knew I was in this bed looking up at you. Is Walter alright?"

"Yes he's fine. He got some burns on the back of his head, but he's already back at work. That was a very brave thing that you did, *Señor* de la Cruz. You saved a man's life. I will see that the Company takes very good care of you."

"Do what you can, doctor, but I don't expect very much from the Company. They don't want any cripples around this town. Too many cripples would show how dangerous their work is."

Doctor Murrieta noticed that the man spoke matter-of-factly, without any bitterness, even though he had suffered a terrible injury.

Four weeks passed by unremarkably, until the day that Doctor Murrieta went on his rounds on the second floor of the hospital. He had looked forward to chatting with Juan de la Cruz, but where Juan had been, he saw only an empty bed. He went to the head nurse to find out where Juan had been moved. He was stunned when she told him that Juan had been discharged.

"Why that is impossible! He is in no condition to be discharged! I gave no orders for his discharge! You had better give me a good explanation!"

The nurse sighed tiredly and then said, "Mr. Clarkston came very early this morning and told me to prepare him for discharge. I told him that I could not do that without your permission, Doctor, but he said that he was ordering me to do so. Then he took him away. What could I do?"

Doctor Murrieta's face turned red, and his eyebrows frowned closer together, which made his face look fierce. He raised his voice, but he was still under control. He said, "From now on, you do not, I repeat, do not discharge anybody without orders from me! I am the doctor here! What does Mr. Clarkston know about medicine? This is not to happen ever again! Do I make myself clear?"

The nurse's face expressed bewilderment, and something else, perhaps resignation. She started to say something, but then thought better of it, and said simply, "Yes, Doctor."

By that time, Doctor Murrieta was out the door and headed for Mr. Clarkston's office. The doctor ignored the "Good morning, Doctor" of Mr. Clarkston's receptionist, brushing past her and flinging open the door to his office, without knocking.

"You have no right to discharge my patients! They are my responsibility, and I, I, say when they can be discharged. Their discharge is a medical decision that is mine alone to make!"

Mr. Clarkston remained sitting behind his large desk that was clear, except for the document he had been working on. He remained calm, as if this sort of thing happened every day.

He said, "Please sit down, you are obviously upset."

"I have never been more upset in my life! I demand to know why you think that you can discharge my patients without even consulting me!"

"You seem to forget, Doctor, that I am the assistant general manager, and that I have full authority over the mine, the smelter, and of course the hospital."

"That cannot be! You are not a doctor! I demand to see the general manager, Mr. Assistant!"

"You can't see him. He is in Montana at this time, and he is rarely here, so I am in charge."

"I want to see the owner then!"

"The general manager and the owner are one and the same person. You will have to deal with me."

"Then you, Mr. Assistant General Manager, will have to give me the explanation and make the changes that I demand!"

"Doctor, you are not in a position to demand anything! You work in a hospital that was built and is staffed by the Company. You live in a house that belongs to the Company, and is built on a Company mining claim. You are paid better than most doctors anywhere, by our Company. You eat the food that is brought here by our Company, over the Company railroad. Don't you see that you are not in a position to demand anything?"

With a slight change in tone, he continued, "It is very obvious, Doctor, that Mr. de la Cruz is of no further use to the Company and never will be. According to Company rules, he is no longer eligible for your services because he is no longer an employee of our Company. You see, we made an inquiry into the accident, and determined that he caused the accident and was injured by his own negligence. Therefore he has been discharged from our employment."

"That cannot be! Juan told me that he was merely doing as he was told by the foreman! When the foreman said, 'tap,' Juan tapped. The foreman should be held responsible. Has the foreman been fired also?"

"Doctor, I have made a thorough inquiry, quite thorough. The foreman told me that he never gave the order to tap, because he knew that the safety procedures had not been finished. There is no doubt who was responsible."

"That is not what Juan de la Cruz told me!"

"Tell me Doctor Murrieta, whom would you have me believe, the foreman or a Mexican laborer?"

"But you did not even talk to Juan de la Cruz!"

"Would it have made any difference if I had?"

Doctor Murrieta knew that he was beaten, and that further argument was futile. But still he asked, "How can you so heartlessly turn out a man to die like that?"

"Now, Doctor, that man was alive, if not well, when we discharged him with the suggestion that he seek medical help on his own."

"I suppose you expect him to find medical help within walking distance, assuming he could walk!"

He spun around in a fury, and slammed the door on his way out. But before the door closed, he heard Mr. Clarkston say, "You will never work again anywhere in this territory!"

An hour later, Doctor Murrieta found the house of Juan de la Cruz, down in the Mexican part of town. Juan was sitting in his yard, in a chair facing the sun, with his legs propped up on a wooden bench. He was throwing scraps of food to the chickens around his chair. Even from several feet away, even with the animal smells in the yard, Doctor Murrieta picked up the smell of rotten meat that was coming from Juan's leg. The gangrene had already started.

Doctor Murrieta approached Juan de la Cruz and said to him, in Spanish, "Juan, I came to say goodbye and to shake the hand of a very brave man."

"You, a doctor, speak Spanish!" Juan exclaimed. "You are leaving?"

"Yes, Juan. I would stay if I could but I cannot work any longer for this kind of a company."

"What a pity, but I understand. Neither am I surprised. You don't look like the other doctors who stayed longer, but they became not much better than butchers. It is a pity that you can't stay. Where are you going? What will you do?"

"At this point I don't know. I'm just going away from here."

"Well, you are lucky, more lucky than I, because you can leave. For me, nothing is left but to face the hard part." He looked down at his leg.

Doctor Murrieta heard what Juan de la Cruz had said, but he made no immediate reply, as he seemed to be lost in thought. He came to an internal decision, and then spoke slowly, choosing his words very carefully.

"Juan," he said, "I am going to leave some pills with you. You may need them if the pain gets to be more than you can stand. But I strongly caution you that if you take too many pills at one time, you could die very quickly."

Before speaking, the doctor had been considering another line of the Hippocratic Oath, the line that followed, "Never do harm to anyone." It said, "I will not give a lethal drug to anyone if I am asked, nor will I advise such a plan."

Doctor Murrieta had come to terms with himself when he took note that Juan had not asked him for the medicine, nor was he as a doctor advising use of the pills, but was in fact cautioning against their use.

"I thank you very much, my friend. I am very grateful to you," said Juan, looking directly into the doctor's eyes. "But you must have another name other than Doctor. Please tell me your name, so that I may wish you a proper farewell."

"My name is Antonio Joaquin Murrieta."

"Don't tell me that you are related to Joaquin Murrieta, the bandit?"

"Juan, he was not a bandit. Nor was he killed by the men who claimed the reward for his life. He was my grandfather."

"Ay," replied Juan de la Cruz. "I am so sorry that you are leaving. We could have had so much to talk about. I worked in the mines of California before I came here. Now all I can do is speed you on your way. You say that you don't know where you are going? Well, just follow the creek there, it is called Bitter Creek. Follow it about four miles down to the river, then turn downstream, and that will lead you to the fort of the soldiers. They will take care of you. May you go with God, good doctor!"

Juan watched as the figure of Doctor Murrieta, carrying only his medical satchel, grew smaller and then was lost from sight around a bend of Bitter Creek.

Town Ordinance No. 2

The Mayor and common council of the town of Jerome do ordain as follows:

Sec 1. Any person violating any of the provisions of the ordinance shall be deemed guilty of a misdemeanor and be punished by a fine not exceeding three hundred dollars or imprisonment not exceeding three months; or, by both such fine and imprisonment.

Section 26. No person who is diseased, maimed, mutilated or in any way deformed, so as to be unsightly or disgusting object or an improper person, to be allowed in or on the streets, highways, thoroughfares or public places in this Town, shall not therein or thereon expose himself or herself to public view.

Signed into effect by William Munds, mayor.
March 21, 1899.

Town Ordinance No. V.

The Mayor and common council of the town of Jerome do ordain as follows:

Sec 1. Any person violating any of the provisions of this ordiance shall be deemed guilty of a misdemeanor and be punished by a fine not exceeding three hundred dollars, or imprisonment not exceeding three months, or; by both such fine and imprisonment,

Section 26. Any person who is diseased, maimed, mutilated or in any way deformed, so as to be unsightly or disgusting object or an improper person to be allowed in or on the streets, highways, thoroughfares or public or public places in this Town, shall not therein or thereon expose himself or herself to public view.

Copy of the 1899 Jerome Town Ordinance. Courtesy of The Jerome Historical Society, Jerome, Arizona.

Juan of the Slag Pots

Juan of the slag pots, sullen and grim,
Scarred of jaw and crooked of limb:
May the Mother of Christ have thought of him!
Ay! Juan, lame Juan—no saint indeed
But a better thing—a man at need.
Night long where the reek of the sulphur smoke
Rolls up till the heart is like to choke;
Till the ears are sick with the clang and whirr,
And the eyeballs ache with the fiery blur,
Juan rolled the slag pots, huge and black,
And poured them out in a burning track
Down the slippery dump like a lava flow,
To cool in the canyon depths below.

Behind in the smelter vast and dim
The beat of the great blast called to him,
And deep in the throat of the furnace glowed
The molten ore on its fiery road;
Soon to flow in a golden stream,
With rainbow shimmer and jeweled gleam
Into the pots like some strange wine.
"Tap!"—The foreman gave the sign
Juan poised the bar on his arm at rest
And swung it straight for the clay-soaked "breast."
A touch—fury of blinding light—

"Back!" The frightened men surged back—
Reeled and ran—but the hindmost fell
Straight in the path of that molten hell.
Cheeks that were black with the stinging smoke
Went white beneath, and a hoarse shout broke
From the swaying crowd—but no man moved;
And the hot flood crept and crawled, and shoved
Its flame-tongues out. Then straight and swift
Juan leaped, and they saw him stoop and lift
A fear-dazed burden, and turn and call
On the saints for mercy. Ay! that's all.
Where the great blasts beat and the smoke drifts low,
Like ragged veils swing to and fro,
Shifting, shimmering, dun and gray,
Juan sits in the sunshine day by day;
Juan of the slag pots, sullen and grim,
Scarred of jaw and crooked of limb—
May the Mother of Christ have thought of him!

Sharlot's note: This poem was suggested by the story of a "run-away" in the old smelter at Jerome in the early days of the United Verde mine. The dumping of the big iron pots of molten slag down into the canyon was one of the weirdly beautiful things to be seen in the old camp, especially at night.

The deep golden glow from the cooling slag could be seen far away on the rim of the Red Rocks and even up on the Mogollones on very dark nights.

by Sharlot Hall

Courtesy of Sharlot Hall Museum, Prescott, Arizona.

Miss Chalmers

I remember one day in September of 1939 because of two things that happened. The first thing that happened was that I kicked a football over the fence at our grammar school, called Building C. The second thing that happened was that some kids got to go see the movie, *Gone with the Wind*, and some kids didn't.

That morning, our usual group of boys was playing touch football before the start of class. I was trying extra hard to kick the football farther than my small physique would allow, so of course the ball veered off to one side and over an eight-foot fence that kept us from falling down the steep hillside. As the ball sailed over the fence, my friend Pete Jauregui immediately started to climb the fence to retrieve the ball. He was the largest and best-developed of our group. As he started over, he looked at me, and I expected to see some reproach in his glance, but there was nothing of the sort. That was typical of Pete. Being largest, he had the power to say or do or look anyway he wanted to, at least with respect to the rest of us. But Pete was a gentle giant, and he always conducted himself as a peace-maker, rather than a bully.

Pete climbed the fence with no difficulty, and went down the hill to retrieve the ball. As he was starting back, we all heard the familiar sound of our teacher's car, and all went to the fence to warn Pete.

"Hurry, Pete. She's coming!"

Pete started up the hill shouting, "Where is she now?"

"Hurry! Her car's coming through town!"

Pete scrambled faster. "Where is she now?" he shouted back.

"She's through town now. She's by the Jerome Transfer curve!"

Although Pete was trying his best to hurry, we were all afraid that he would not get back on the playground before Miss Chalmers arrived.

We followed her progress by the sound of an automobile engine screaming at its maximum rpm like a race car. Judging strictly by the sound, you would have guessed that the car had to be traveling at least a hundred miles an hour. However, because Miss Chalmers always kept her car in the first, the lowest gear, her car was only moving at about twenty-five miles per hour. She always drove in first gear, because, as she told her class, "Those higher gears are the ones in which people get killed."

She always drove slowly, with the engine screaming, so it was not a problem to follow her progress from her home in the United Verde Apartments, along Main Street through the business district, downhill past the Jerome Transfer and the Methodist Church, past the Union Meat Market, to the level area where the school was located.

Because Jerome was built on the side of a mountain, and the main part of town was higher than our school, the sound of Miss Chalmer's car carried very well. The sound of the screaming car ricocheted down the mountain every school day, once in the morning, as she drove to school, and again in the evening when she drove home. People had gotten so accustomed to it that not even the miners, who had gone to bed only a few hours before, were awakened by her passing.

Miss Chalmers pulled into the school playground in her black Buick coupe. Her car had a spare tire mounted on each front fender covered with black metal that exactly matched the color of the car. It was a very sporty car, the envy of not just the school boys, but many grown men as well.

Miss Chalmers drove slowly near the edge of the playground, along the fence, back towards where she parked her car. When she saw Pete Jauregi on a level with her eyes, on the outside of the fence, she stopped her car and glared at him.

Pete was spread-eagled, with his hands still two feet from the top of the fence, his legs spread apart, his toes showing through his old shoes that were worn out, too small for him, his feet lodged in the steel mesh fence.

When Miss Chalmers stopped her car, Pete froze. He and the teacher locked eyes, and for a moment, neither moved. Then Miss Chalmers reached over to the passenger's side, rolled down the window and said in her customary teacher's voice that commanded respect and obedience, "Pete, get into this playground right now, and go sit in my classroom! I will deal with you later!"

Pete said nothing to Miss Chalmers in reply. Not because he was afraid, but because of his gentle manner of dealing with adults as well as children. Because he was several years older than his classmates, he was correspondingly bigger and stronger, and far more advanced emotionally. His father had been killed in the mine two years before, which left his family without money; too poor to leave Jerome, too poor to stay. Since the father's death, the family had been struggling to survive with the help of neighbors and friends. Pete and his siblings had stayed out of school for a time, and did what they could do to help.

Pete chopped firewood for his neighbors, who paid as they were able, with some firewood or a nickel or a dime, which Pete passed on to his mother. But it was obvious that the family was barely making it, because Pete came to school with worn-out shoes, wearing shirts that were too small for him, and pants that were too big.

Those two years out of school taught Pete a lot about life. He was always grateful for any favor from anyone, and of course that made everyone try harder to help him. "Here, Pete. I'm not very hungry. Please take this half of a sandwich that I can't eat, etc." These circumstances had formed Pete's gentleness and humility, so that he was well-liked by everyone.

Everyone except Miss Chalmers. I remember the first day Pete came into her class. She asked him his name, and he replied, "Pedro Jauregui."

She said, "Pedro what?"

"Pedro Jauregui."

"I can't pronounce a name like that! I am just going to call you Pete. If I say 'Pete,' you answer. Do you understand?"

"Yes, ma'am."

After that, Miss Chalmers always used a little harsher tone of voice with Pete than with her other pupils, and she was always a little harder and more strict with him than with anyone else.

By this time, Miss Chalmers was already a "fixture"

at Building C. She taught fifth and sixth grades in alternate years. Her reputation as a strict disciplinarian had been long established, and even some third graders knew of her, and were afraid that they would wind up in her class when they got older. I learned later that she came from a rich family in San Francisco. She must have had some money other than her salary as a teacher, because no one else in town could afford to drive a car like hers, much less on a teacher's salary.

After I grew up, I wondered why she had come to Jerome. She had come when she was in the prime of her life, and I am certain that she did not come to Jerome to wind up an old-maid school teacher. Most probably she had done some homework, and learned that Jerome had thousands of single men who worked in the mine. But what she probably did not know before she arrived is that the single miners were a rough lot, mostly uneducated, and although unbelievably brave in their work, even those actively seeking a wife would have been too terrified to approach her. After all, Miss Chalmers was college educated, and was a *teacher.*

Miss Chalmers had passed her prime alone, and now she spent her middle age alone, teaching. When she was not teaching, she spent her time with other single teachers who also lived in the United Verde Apartments. They had their own social life, so that if in the evening they got a knock on their door, they would ask, "Who is it?" If the response was, "It is I," they would open the door, knowing that it was another teacher. If the response was, "It's me," they knew to inquire further before opening the door.

Miss Chalmers had settled into her middle age. She wore black to make herself look slimmer, and was constantly struggling to keep her weight down, but she had lost the struggle. The pudgy skin of her forearms hung over her wrists, and her calves over her ankles.

Her hair had thinned on the top near the back, so she wore a bun made of hair that did not match her own. At lunchtime, she never left the classroom, and her lunch always consisted of Melba toast and a quart can of pineapple juice. Still, she was a commanding figure. Her round, wire-rimmed glasses magnified her eyes, so she could freeze any pupil with just a look.

After the school bell ended the playground games, all the pupils sat in her classroom for their first class, in penmanship. Miss Chalmers emphasized that good writing was formed by the wrist that produced smooth, sweeping, pleasing letters. Too much use of the fingers produced tense, stilted writing. Miss Chalmers assigned a paragraph to be copied twenty times by each student. She waited until a pupil was absorbed in writing out the assigned sentences, and then she would suddenly reach out to take the pencil from the pupil's grasp. If the pencil came out easily, she was satisfied. If the pencil did not release easily, she would whack the student on the hand with her ruler. When she tested Pete's pencil, he was holding it too tightly.

Pete was still expecting his punishment, so of course he was tense. Miss Chalmers did not say anything; she just whacked his hand a little harder than usual, and went on to the next pupil.

The next classes were reading, arithmetic and geography. After that, it was time for lunch. The students who had lunch money were excused to go to the cafeteria for a hot lunch. The rest stayed in their seats and ate lunches from home. Those students who had sandwiches on white bread spread their lunches on their desks; those who had beans or potatoes wrapped in a tortilla kept their tortilla in their brown paper bag, and only took it out to nibble a bite.

Miss Chalmers as usual ate her lunch at her desk. I sat close enough to her desk that when she poured out that stream of yellow, golden pineapple juice into her glass, I could smell it. That was enough to transport me to dreaming of tropical islands where the weather was always warm, where there were fountains of free pineapple juice. I dreamed that one day she would offer me a taste of juice, but that never happened. I also dreamed of having a whole quart of pineapple juice to take home. We would have made the quart last a week by drinking tiny portions at a time.

When the lunch period was over and the students had come back from the cafeteria, Miss Chalmers addressed the class and said, "I am sure that you have not forgotten that today you will be allowed to skip this afternoon's classes, including our history class, to attend the special matinee of *Gone With the Wind* that the Ritz Theatre is having for all our students. The movie is entirely filmed in that new Technicolor. The movie covers the Civil War that we have been studying about, so it is very appropriate for our history class. I have seen it, and it is an excellent movie, so I know that you will like it."

Then she gave her instructions. "Please come to my desk, one at a time, one row at a time, starting with the row nearest the windows. First turn in your homework assignment to me, then give me your quarter. I will give you your ticket, and you can leave for the movie. For those of you who choose not to go to the movie, please turn in your homework and return to your seats. You can memorize President Lincoln's *Gettysburg Address* until it is time to go home, at your usual time."

All the "American" kids left their homework and their quarter at her desk then went out the door. The "Mexican" kids left their homework at her desk, then returned to their desks, because they did not have a quarter for the movie. The last American boy, who lived in The Gulch where most of the residents were Mexican, went out the door with a look in his eyes that said, "I may be poor, but I am not as poor as you are!"

After the movie-goers had left, Miss Chalmers noted that Pete Jauregui had not turned in his homework. She stood up so abruptly that her chair made a scraping sound on the floor. She walked officiously to Pete's desk, crossed her arms in front of her chest, and asked, "And where is your homework?"

Pete said, in a timid but respectful voice, "I'm sorry, Miss Chalmers, but I couldn't do it last night."

"Why not? You knew very well that it was due today! Young man, with that escapade on the fence this morning, and now this, I am quickly losing my patience with you!"

"I couldn't do it, teacher. There was a full moon last night."

"Now I am really losing my patience! What does a full moon have to do with your homework?"

"Teacher, we don't have any lights in my house, so I have to do my homework by the light of the street lamp. When there is a full moon, the town does not turn on its street lights. I just couldn't see well enough to do it last night. I tried. I'm sorry."

"Don't you have a kerosene lamp?"

"No."

"No candles?"

"No."

Miss Chalmers quickly spun around to return to her desk, but I could see that she was trying to compose herself. She sat silently for a few moments with her head down. Then she raised her head and looked at the brown faces of all the pupils who had not been able to attend the movie that afternoon. Then, in a softer tone of voice than I had ever heard her use, she said, "*Pedro,* why don't you and the rest of the class come with me to the music room? I will play some music for you."

King Copper

A very powerful man was C.W. Holley, and he knew it. He was not physically powerful to look at, but his economic power was almost absolute in Jerome. Very few people even knew his given name, and nearly all of those who did know it would never have dared to use it. He was always "Mr. Holley" to his subordinates. And everyone in this isolated, remote town of Jerome, Arizona, in the Black Hills Mining District, was his subordinate.

As general manager of the Company, Mr. Holley answered only to the Senator. The Senator was the actual and sole owner of the entire mine, its smelter, and the railroad that connected Jerome to the main line at Ash Fork. On his infrequent and unannounced visits to Jerome, the Senator rarely stayed longer than necessary to make a personal visual inspection of the surface and underground workings and ask a few incisive questions, mostly pertaining to the extent and purity of the ore body of high grade copper. The copper contained enough gold and silver to pay for the mine's operating expenses. That left the value of the extracted copper as pure profit for the Senator.

The Senator called Mr. Holley "Charlie." He trusted Mr. Holley to the point that he never questioned Mr. Holley's operational decisions. That left Mr. Holley free to use the power that came with running one of the two large mining companies in the State of Arizona. The other company, the Queen, was in the southern part of the state, near the border with Mexico. Since the two companies acted cooperatively for their mutual benefit, between them they controlled the economic power of Arizona.

Jerome was so remote that aside from the Little Daisy Mine in Jerome that was owned by the Douglas family, there was no other place of any size in which to work that was closer than a two-day journey. It was well known that a miner discharged by the Company would find that the Little Daisy did not need a new miner that day, or the next day, or the next week, or the week after that. Even the most determined miner would soon get the message that there was not, nor would there ever be, any more work for him in Jerome. That of course added to Mr. Holley's power.

Mr. Holley was well versed in history, and he thought that his power was like the men in the Council of Ten in medieval Venice, who had the power to determine who could live in Venice, who could work there, what kind of work they could do, whom they could marry, and who would die, if the Council decided.

His employees knew what they were supposed to do, and as long as they performed well, everything went along quite smoothly. While he had no close friends, he was always treated with respect, although there was always a touch of fear present. He had many acquaintances at work, of course, in the town itself, in the Lodge, and in the Episcopal Church where he attended services every Sunday, seated in his reserved pew with his wife and two children, a boy and a girl nearing their teen-age years.

On Lodge nights, he would walk from his home on Company Hill, the best house in Jerome not counting the Douglas Mansion, which Mr. Holley thought ostentatious, even for an owner of a mine. Mr. Holley contented himself with the thought that his own house, which he considered to be his own, although it did in fact belong to the Company, had a more commanding view of the town and the Verde Valley, all the way to Sedona.

Life was good for Mr. Holley. Nevertheless, one day he realized that he no longer took pleasure in being greeted, "Good morning, Mr. Holley. Good evening, Mr. Holley. How do you do, Mr. Holley?"

In fact, the only time he paid attention to the omission of "How do you do, Mr. Holley?" was when he passed one of the young girls from the House of Miss Lilly on the street. Invariably, they would lower their eyes and pass him without a word. If they would at least make eye contact! But he knew that eye contact was the only kind of contact that he could hope to have with them. He could imagine the scandal that would follow if he ever actually patronized the House of Miss Lilly. Why this entire town would hear about it before he even finished putting his pants back on!

No, such a scandal would never be tolerated in Jerome, especially involving someone of his importance.

"I have to keep reminding myself of this," he thought to himself. "I can't let my longings jeopardize my position with the Company. I can't expose myself or my family to a scandal. How would I ever face them?"

He had had several of these bouts of self-recrimination, for he had finally succumbed to temptation—though not to any of Miss Lilly's girls. He was embroiled in a secret affair with Miss Lorry, an employee in his office. "I must end this before I get any deeper than I already am," he thought to himself.

Their relationship had begun innocently enough, as a favor to the principal of the high school, who had told Mr. Holley that one of his good and deserving students desperately needed a job to help support her mother and younger sisters. The principal said that the family had been surviving on the mother's work cleaning houses and taking in wash for other people. The principal had said that the work was unseemly for a white woman, and that kind of work should be left to foreigners.

Mr. Holley agreed with him, and inquired if the girl was honest and good with figures. He hired her sight unseen as an assistant to his timekeeper in the accounting office. As often happens, however, innocent beginnings develop a life of their own.

When Miss Lorry had first come in to his office with the timekeeping reports, he was flustered, but felt a strong need to make himself look important. He felt his temperature rise, yet tried to appear calm. His breathing became more rapid, but he was able to convey the appearance of being totally in self control. His emotions were in conflict. He tried to look younger and more fatherly all at the same time. All because of a petite creature with blue eyes, straight black hair to her shoulders, with fair skin that made her black hair seem darker.

Mr. Holley thought, "Words cannot capture the essence that God has put into a young woman at the peak of her beauty."

When Miss Lorry said, "Good morning, Mr. Holley," and got no response she thought that the poor man must have many weighty things on his mind. She repeated, "Good morning, Mr. Holley." Mr. Holley then brought his attention back to the moment, and he was able to respond.

Some time after their relationship had progressed and the bonds of their entanglement strengthened, Mr. Holley tried to explain to himself why she had such a strong effect on him. It is doubtful that these things can ever be rationally explained, but rational minds like Mr. Holley's want an explanation. He adopted the explanation that Miss Lorry reminded him of the love whom he had rejected, to chase a relationship with more economic and social advantages.

In retrospect, Mr. Holley could see that his first mistake was to have left his desk to sit on the leather couch in his office, and invite Miss Lorry to sit next to him while she made her report. She sat close enough to him that he could smell the young, clean scent of the woman's body next to him. As she finished her report, he thanked her and patted her knee. He told himself that it was a fatherly pat, but he did not fail to note how good it felt to him, and how she did not withdraw. Maybe if she had drawn away at that point, things would have gone no further. Did Miss Lorry not withdraw because she needed the job? Because she was afraid of him? Because she needed affection? Mr. Holley would never know the answer. But indeed things did go further, as they usually do between a powerful man and a vulnerable woman.

After that, Mr. Holley assigned other duties to her, so that she would have more reasons to come into his office, and the leather couch. But pleasure has its price, which constantly escalates. Now, after three months of pleasure had passed, Mr. Holley felt that the price was too high, and decided that he would break off the affair at the first good opportunity.

He thought that the first good opportunity would be on Monday, after they came back to work from the

Fourth of July holiday. He would tell her that everything was over, but only after he had completed his important meeting with mine owner, James Douglas, scheduled that same morning. He expected a favorable outcome from the meeting, and he knew that the rush of adrenaline after his successful negotiations would give him the strength to break off his relationship. He did not expect it to be easy, but he had no idea that it would be so difficult.

On Monday morning, Mr. Holley arrived at his office early. Promptly at eight o'clock, Mr. Douglas was ushered in.

"Good morning, Jimmy. How are things in Little Mexico?" This was an allusion to the fact that Mr. Douglas used many miners from Mexico in the Little Daisy mine.

"*Van muy bien.* Except that my miners are so good that they are mining so much gold and silver that I may have to change my smelting process. But tell me, how are things going in *La Mina Grande*?"

"The Big Mine's doing well. Can't complain. We still can't find the bottom of our ore body. If things keep going like they are, I am going to have to start learning Chinese, in case we have to negotiate apex rights with China."

"Speaking of apex rights, isn't that what we are here for this morning?"

"Of course, Jimmy. But will you have some refreshment with me while we're talking? Please, have a seat," he said, gesturing to the couch.

When Miss Lorry brought in the tray, Mr. Holley saw that her eyes were red from crying. She tried not to let him see, but Mr. Holley saw enough to make him wonder how she had known in advance that today he was going to break things off. Nevertheless, he kept his mind on the business at hand.

When Jimmy saw the tray of Mexican pastries and Mexican chocolate, he said, "Charlie, you have put me on my guard. Is this going to be the most expensive *pan dulce* and chocolate that I have ever had, or what?"

"No, Jimmy. There's a greater advantage for both of us if we simply agree not to start suing each other over whether our underground ore bodies are within our surface claims, whether the ore bodies were continuous or not, whether your claims were junior or senior to ours, all those kinds of issues."

Jimmy said, "I'll make it easy for you, Charlie. Of course I will agree to forego apex litigation with you. I'm no fool. Working with you on the Hull claims showed me that we are both way better off if we cooperate, instead of fighting with each other. You and I both know what happened at the Tom King Mine over in Oatman. Their apex fights went all the way to the Supreme Court, and about eight years worth of good gold production went into the pockets of the lawyers. Do you think that I want any part of that?"

"Jimmy, you make it too easy for me. You must be getting soft in your old age. But if we've got an agreement, then let me call my underground shift boss right away."

Picking up his telephone, he kept his finger hidden on the cradle, so that no connection was actually made. Faking a phone call, he said, "Conn, you know that raise that I told you to give your full attention to? Yes, that one. The vertical raise from the drift that connects the Hopewell Tunnel to the Texas Shaft. Yes, the one that would hit the surface under the Douglas Mansion. That one. Well you can forget about punching into the Douglas' living room. That's right, shut it down completely, you got that? Never mind why, just shut it down."

Then turning directly to Jimmy, he said, "Don't

worry, Jimmy. Before we would have broken through to your living room, we would have given you plenty of notice so that neither you nor your French guests would have been disturbed. See what nice people we are?"

Jimmy responded in a similar bantering tone of voice, "Charlie, I know that the reputation of ruthlessness that you and your company both have is over-rated and undeserved, once in a while, anyway. I know that underneath that hard exterior there beats a heart of pure copper. So before I came over here this morning, I too shut down my operation under your big house on Company Hill. Not that we were that close to breaking surface, but we were close enough to rattle your fine china. So if we have reached a détente, as we say in French, why don't we enjoy these pastries?"

After Mr. Douglas left, Mr. Holley could not restrain his elation. The Senator would be very pleased that there would be no need to set aside a few million dollars for potential apex litigation. He would be especially pleased that the matter had been settled so amicably. Of course Mr. Holley would be given a great deal of credit for the agreement. A big raise, perhaps?

His reverie was short lived when Miss Lorry burst unannounced into the room, not even trying to hold back her tears. She blubbered, "Charlie, I have to talk to you."

That brought the matter of Miss Lorry back to his consciousness with a blow to his stomach. His self-congratulatory dreaming was shattered by the realization that he could lose everything as a result of his own weakness. How could he have ever let things get so far out of control? His resolve to end the affair was strengthened. He said to her, "I agree that we have to talk. But first, tell me what's wrong?"

"I'm pregnant," she said through more tears.

Mr. Holley felt the bottom drop out of his world. Could life have such a heart of copper that it would let him glimpse the sweetness of a future of great promise, then immediately shatter it and replace it with the bitterness of disgrace and despair? He had to sit down. He sat in the chair behind his desk, not on the leather couch. Miss Lorry was so emotional that she took no note of the change. She did not stop sobbing until Mr. Holley was forced to put his arms around her to calm her down.

He told her, "Please, honey. Try to compose yourself. We can't let anyone know that there is anything wrong. As soon as you have gotten yourself together, go back to your work as if nothing has changed. Come back at quitting time, and by then I will have figured out what to do. I can't even think with you in here crying."

When she returned, he told her that he had made a phone call, and that he had a good solution. She said, "I knew that you would know what to do."

"We have to act fast," said Mr. Holley. "We will check you in right away to the Company hospital. The surgeon will do anything that I ask of him, and we won't need to worry about any of this getting out. He can say that he removed an ovarian cyst, and no one will question him. Trust me, everything will be all right." Mr. Holley expected to see a look of relief on her face, but instead he saw a fresh flood of tears that caught him by surprise.

He asked, "What's wrong? Don't you trust me?"

She could not tell him that all afternoon she had been dreaming that he would divorce his wife, that they would raise their child together along with the other children that would come along, that she would become the new Copper Queen of Jerome. His proposed solution had totally crushed her dreams.

Mr. Holley asked her again if she could check into the Company hospital the next morning, but she did not answer him immediately. She took some time to formulate a reply, and in that moment she transformed herself from a complacent, compliant young woman into a woman fully possessed of her strength.

Her reply was very firm. "No, I will not consent to an abortion! I absolutely will not! I want to have your baby because it is a part of you, a part of us!"

Now it was Mr. Holley's turn to have his dreams crushed. He knew that he was facing disgrace, dismissal, and loss of his prestige and family. He was aware that he was no longer in control and was subject to the wishes of the young lady in front of him. But he was perceptive enough to realize that if he tried to impose his will, he would surely lose. He decided that the best tactic was to retreat and reorganize.

He embraced her and said, "Honey, I will respect your wish. But give me some time to think about the best way to proceed. Come to work tomorrow, and I will call you in if I can think of something we can do."

That night Mr. Holley deflected all questions from his family about his troubled appearance. He said that he had had a difficult day at the office, without mentioning his coup with James Douglas. He went to bed early, but could not sleep until he found a solution that might keep his life from shattering. One option that he considered only briefly was taking his own life, but he dismissed it quickly because he realized that even that act would not save his family. He did not fall asleep until he saw the light of a new day.

In spite of his lack of sleep, when he entered his office at the usual time, he was the pre-Miss Lorry top executive: clear-minded, self-possessed and totally in control. He called Miss Lorry into his office, and told her, "I am going to accommodate your wish to give birth to our child because I am truly honored that you would want to do that. But you must never disclose to anyone that I am the true father of your child. I will see that you and your husband will always have good jobs with the Company, and you will see to it that our child is well raised. There will be nothing more between us. You must do everything that I tell you to do. You have no options, and you do not even want to know the consequences if you refuse."

She interrupted, "But I don't even have a husband!"

"You will have, this very morning. Come into my office at eleven this morning, and you will have a number of good, eligible men to choose from. Choose the man that you want for your husband. Be a good and faithful wife to him and raise the child. Understood? You can leave now, we have nothing more to discuss."

"But what if he doesn't like me?"

"He will like you. Leave that to me."

She left with her face as pale as dust, as though life had drained from her. As soon as she left, Mr. Holley called his shift boss. "Sullivan, I want you to have a dozen of your men in my office at eleven o'clock this morning. No, they are not being fired; you don't need to know what I want them for. Just have them here. I want only single men between twenty-five and thirty years old. No underground men. I don't want them tracking their mud in my office. Oh yes, only Englishmen or Irishmen, no other races. Don't dock their time. This is on my orders if anybody asks, but nobody should ask, understood?"

The men came in at the appointed time, looking nervously at the wood paneling, the rich leather couch and chairs, but mostly they looked at the big walnut desk and the man behind it. They acted as if they expected to be fired, and each wondered what they had done wrong. They also looked boldly at the attractive young woman in the office. They were still wondering what it was all about, even when all of them, all but one man, returned to their jobs.

Miss Lorry had signaled to Mr. Holley with her eyes to indicate the man she had selected. Consciously or unconsciously she had chosen the man who most closely resembled Mr. Holley, only younger. Miss Lorry was told to return to her work, while the man remained alone with Mr. Holley.

The wedding took place a week later, in front of the local Justice of the Peace, who was also a Company man. The bride and groom moved into a newly purchased, modest home on School Street near the Jerome Bakery. Seven months later, a girl was born to the couple. The women said, "She looks just like her father," referring to Lorry's husband. It turned out to be a successful marriage, and four years later, another girl was born to them. The two girls did not look very much alike, but they looked close enough alike to be sisters.

La Crees-ees, Jerome, Arizona 1935

Belia was a mother by the time she was ten years old. Maybe sooner, I don't know. She was my sister and six years older than I, so you can't expect me to have much awareness of things like that. I don't mean she actually gave birth to a child, or anything of that sort. I mean she was like an extra mother to me and my brothers and sisters, especially since my twin sisters had been born four months ago.

They were identical twins, one named Barbara and the other Carolina. Carolina died last month, so only Barbara was left. They were so small that I could hardly believe Belia when she told me that at one time I had been that small, too. The twins cried a lot; it seemed like they cried all the time. But when they stopped crying, you could see that they had well-formed delicate features and would have grown up to be beautiful women like my mother and Belia. But they were too skinny.

I thought that all babies had chubby cheeks, but

my sisters had hardly any meat over their cheekbones, and they looked pale. Come to think of it, my mother and Belia looked like that, too. In fact, we all looked that way. Mother told us often that we needed to be strong, because times were hard, whatever that meant, and that we were in a *crees-ees*, which is what the English word "crisis" sounds like in Spanish.

There was no doubt that we were in a crees-ees, although the word applied to those times was "depression." But we were in no depression, we were in a full-blown crees-ees, although there were plenty of reasons for everyone to be depressed.

The year was 1935. The locale was Jerome, Arizona, a mining town solely dependent on two copper mines: the United Verde, known as The Big Mine (*La Mina Grande*) and the UVX, known as The Little Daisy (*La Day-see*). Both mines had been closed for several years because the price of copper had dropped to 5 cents a pound. There was no other industry, no other work, no other jobs. Everyone in town depended on the mines, and without their payrolls, everyone was reduced to the bare essentials of food, sex and alcohol. Sex was reduced to wishful thinking; alcohol was reduced to homemade beer and wine. The real problem was food.

Jerome was situated in a place where you could not grow your own food. In Jerome, the top layer of earth was not topsoil. You would have to say that it was top-rocks. The hard *caliche* dirt was filled with hundreds of rocks where no earthworms could penetrate to make topsoil. The rocks ranged from the size of a BB to rocks so big that you could not move them unless you blew them apart with dynamite. You could not grow a carrot or a potato; food had to come from somewhere else.

In those years, there was no unemployment compensation, there was no welfare. To survive, you needed cash, or credit if you could get it. The only thing that kept Jerome alive was that the mine kept a few men employed as caretakers, in case the price of copper went up again so that the mines could re-open. With the price of copper at 5 cents per pound, it could not go much lower. Without the caretaker employees, the town would have been abandoned. The only government assistance was when a relief truck chugged into the municipal yard and the driver handed out small bags of flour. If Marie Antoinette would have been in Jerome in 1935 she would have said, "Let them eat flour tortillas!"

At this time, many houses were without electricity because the occupants had no money to pay their electricity bills. Because hurricane lamps burning kerosene or coal oil were much cheaper than electricity, people used them. At night, Jerome would appear almost totally dark.

At least the drinking water was free, but unless you had bread to go with the water, it was not very nourishing. Wood was still needed to heat the stoves for cooking and for heating the house. Fortunately, in August the houses did not need heating. But in the winter, with snow on the ground and on the roofs, with icicles two inches in diameter hanging from the eaves, it was necessary for everyone to huddle close to the stove for warmth, for that was the only source of heat. Because firewood was so precious, it commanded a good price. The wood had to be brought from thirty to forty miles away. All the local trees had been cut down decades ago for mine timbers.

The wood was sold by woodcutters who delivered the two-foot logs with the bark still on. It had to be chopped into smaller pieces that would fit into the stove. That job fell to boys who were strong enough and careful enough to swing a hand axe.

During the crees-ees, the men of the house were

doing whatever they could to enable their families to survive. The hunters went hunting for deer, but venison was not easy to come by. Some men went panning for gold in Lynx Creek near Prescott, but most placers had been picked clean for quite some time. Other men spent their time collecting dry brush for the cooking stove, at least enough to cook one meal. The gamblers tried to make money in poker games, but even the gambling rooms had closed down. There were very few dollars circulating, and it was not much fun to play for beans.

Even the self-reliant, low-overhead trader who sold blankets and pots and pans to housewives was hurting. He was a man of Middle-Eastern descent who was known as *"El Viejo Arabe,"* "Old Arab Man." This man sold his goods, mostly blankets, on credit, payable at the rate of 25 cents every payday. But for him, some people would probably have died of pneumonia or frozen to death. However, since there were no more paydays, his business was not doing too well.

One day he came to our house and knocked on the door to collect. My mother did not have the 25 cents that was due, so she told me to answer the door and tell Viejo Arabe that she was not at home. I did exactly as she told me. I told the man, "My mother said to tell you that she is not home."

Even though smiles were not often seen in those times, and even though he needed the money, he managed to smile through his look of disappointment and say, "When your mother comes back, tell her that I will return in two weeks."

He left, slightly bent over, with his hands in his pockets, walking slowly down the hill, murmuring something that I couldn't understand.

When El Viejo Arabe left our house, he walked downhill, for there were no houses uphill from ours. We lived at 517 Giroux Street, on the highest street in

Jerome. When I lay in my bed next to an outside wall, in wintertime I could see snow outside through the cracks between the boards.

Giroux Street was on the southern side, the hospital side, of Jerome. The northern end of Giroux Street had all the nice Victorian houses. That section was known as Company Hill, where the superintendent of the United Verde Mine lived, along with the other big shots of the mine.

Our house had four rooms: a kitchen, a living room and two bedrooms. The best part of our house was the front porch with a view that, without exaggeration, could be called incomparable. The red sandstone rocks of Sedona looked like a cross-section of the Grand Canyon with some of the colors of the Painted Desert, and including, on a smaller scale, the rock formations of Monument Valley. All these combined into one beautiful vista. Our house was built of unpainted weathered lumber, without insulation anywhere, and the cooking stove was the only source of heat for the whole house.

The best feature of the house was its location, up high on the hill. The mining company normally did not permit "Mexican" families to live in the higher elevations of town. We lived up so high because our house was not built on a mining claim owned by the United Verde.

In those days, the term "Mexican-American" had not yet been invented. A Mexican was anyone with brown skin, or a Spanish surname, or whose ancestry traced back to Mexico. It did not matter if a Mexican had been born in the United States, from ancestors who had been born in this country for five generations, he was still a Mexican.

Being considered a Mexican was not very desirable. A Mexican miner received less pay than an "American" miner for the same work, and was assigned to the more dangerous work underground, never on the surface. It was better to be an American who had come from England, Ireland, or Germany. Italians and Slavs, although they were European, were considered somewhere in-between those other two groups.

Mexicans lived in the less desirable parts of Jerome, like Mexican Town, the section downhill from the business section. This area had only a view of the opposite side of a narrow canyon, and it was cold. The ice and snow lingered longest here in the shadow of the canyon. The other area for Mexicans was known as The Gulch. That was also in a canyon, not quite as narrow as the Mexican Town canyon, but it was a thousand feet lower in elevation than Giroux Street. Neither The Gulch nor Mexican Town had a view of the Red Rocks. They were the last parts of town to see the morning sun, and the first parts in shadow.

The Mexicans were not confined to their barrios by any Town ordinance, but by the real law in town: the mining companies. They exercised their power through the unwritten and unspoken rule that Mexicans were not welcome in the parts of town known as the 500-foot level, where the professional employees lived, nor the 300-foot level, where the "Whites Only" swimming pool was located.

Consequently, when my cousin Alex and I wanted to see the explosions at the open pit that took place at 3:00 pm every day, we would walk along Giroux Street, behind the Company Hill houses, crouching low, afraid to be seen by anyone inside.

The view from our front porch provided us with most of our entertainment. Our mother would sit with us outside and gaze at the magnificent rock formations, and we would play on the porch and talk to her. On good days, before she started having trouble with her twin baby girls, we would spend the evening hours on the porch, watching the shadows move across the valley floor until they crossed the Verde River on the other side of Clarkdale.

We continued to watch as the shadows changed the aspect of the Red Rocks every few minutes, and until the sun left the top peaks in darkness. Then we would start watching for a train that looked very small from so far away. The train would leave the Clarkdale smelter, travel the circumference of the slag pile and stop to dump each individual car loaded with molten slag. The slag spilled over the side of the dump, glowing bright yellow at first, then slowly turning into a darker and darker red as it cooled. The glow from the molten slag lighted up the entire mountain on the other side of the Verde River in a red incandescent glow. The train dumped the slag at 9:00 pm, and after the red glow slowly faded to black it was time to go inside to bed.

In earlier times, the whole family, except for our father, would spend a few hours together on the porch almost every day the weather was good. Most of the time we spent quietly watching as the daylight turned to darkness, sometimes talking to each other, sometimes talking to Mama. On occasion, Clarence, the only black boy in town, would come visit my older brother. At other times Irma, our Italian neighbor, would come visit my older sister.

Often we would try to solve riddles such as *"redondito, redondon—que no tiene tapa ni tapon"* (little round, big round—that has neither lid nor stopper). I remember that riddle because I had such a hard time figuring out the answer: a ring. I also remember asking my mother why we were poor. She responded that we were poor, but that we would not always be poor, but that we and everyone else in Jerome were in a crees-ees.

Our family was definitely in a crees-ees. On that

evening in August, 1935, when the first twin, Carolina had been dead a month, Mama sat rocking back and forth with the other twin in her arms. We could hear her murmuring prayers to Barbarita, occasionally pausing for a sad, prolonged sigh. Barbarita had been fussy and crying all evening. When the baby became silent, we knew that they had both fallen asleep. Belia went up close to them, then looked at us with her finger raised to her lips and whispered for silence. Then she checked to see that Barbarita was wrapped in her blanket, and the blanket properly wrapped about Mama's shoulder and arm, so there was no danger of the baby falling.

Belia moved away from them and closer to us before saying, "Be quiet and let them sleep. They are both completely exhausted."

So we sat quietly, again watching the sunlight fade, and the shadows moving towards the Red Rocks of Sedona. But the light was different on this evening. Instead of the normal brilliant yellow of the sun, this sunlight was tinged with brown, making it the color of weak tea. The night before, there had been a ring around the moon, and Mama said that meant that a change was coming. I hoped, I really hoped, that the change was for the better, because the crees-ees couldn't get much worse. I hoped.

Then Belia came to me and whispered, "I want to talk to you." She led me to the far end of the porch. "We have to whisper, because we have to let Mama sleep and get at least a little rest."

She was about to say something else, when I interrupted her to say that I was hungry. With a trace of irritation in her voice, she snapped, "That is exactly what I want to talk to you about! Do you remember when we were eating this afternoon? Do you know why I kicked you under the table?"

Little Boy Lives in a Copper Camp by Lew Davis. Courtesy of Phoenix Art Museum.

"No, but you sure kicked me hard, and you hurt me!"

"You deserved it! I kicked you because you asked for another helping of beans."

"What's wrong with that? I was hungry!"

"I know you were hungry. We are all hungry. But you must not ever do that again, do you understand?"

"What did I do wrong?"

"Well, for one thing, you're too concerned with yourself, and you don't see what is going on!"

"Like what?"

"Don't you see that your brother and I never ask for more, and we always, always leave some food on our plates. We don't eat it all, like you do. I bet that you don't even know why we do that. We do that because we love our mother!"

"I love her too, more than you!"

"You make me so mad sometimes! It's because Mama puts all the food that she has on the plates for us kids, and tries to make the portions equal for everybody. But haven't you noticed that she never sits down with us, that she never sets a plate aside for herself? Because, dummy, she eats only what we leave on our plates! She has nothing, nothing to give you if you ask for more. And what's more, if you don't leave anything on your plate, she doesn't have anything to eat! So from now on, you will make sure that you always leave something on your plate. If she asks you to finish what's on your plate, you tell her that you can't finish because you're too full. Do you understand? I know that you will do it, because you love her as much as we all do.

"But let me tell you something else you can do, and this will really help you. It's kind of a trick. When you get your plate, first set aside a portion for Mama. Then start eating what you have set aside for yourself. But take very small bites of everything, and chew each bite slowly and well. Treat each bite as if it were the last one on your plate, and give it all your attention. Don't let your mind wander from what you are doing, from chewing your food. And do you know what? If you do this, you really will feel full, and you won't have to fin-ish what is on your plate, and you can leave something for Mama. We have to help her because she is so worn out. Don't forget now, so that I don't have to kick you anymore, okay?

"And one more thing. If you do as I have told you, but you are still so hungry that you can't stand it anymore, then come to me when Mama is not looking, and I will give you a tortilla with a little lard spread on it, with a little bit of salt. That makes the lard taste pretty good, and you won't be hungry anymore."

At that point, Barbarita started crying again, and Belia went to help Mama. Shortly after that, we saw the train at the smelter dump the slag, so we all headed for bed. I did not fall asleep right away. I could hear Barbarita crying again, and heard Mama going back and forth with her, from the bedroom to the kitchen. I heard Papa come home, and he usually did not come home before eleven o'clock, so I knew that it was later than that. I heard him say to Mama, "Shut that kid up!"

Mama took Barbarita into the kitchen. I could hear them both crying. After some time I heard Papa snoring, and after that I fell asleep.

The next morning we arose early, because the sun comes over the eastern horizon, the Mogollon Rim, around five o'clock in the morning. Mama had already been up before us, because she had already lit a fire in the wood stove, and had prepared a pot of coffee. We kids were sitting on the benches of a picnic table that served as our dining table, eating our bowls of beans. As we were finishing eating, Papa came into the kitchen and washed his face in the kitchen sink, for that was the only plumbing in the house. He smoothed back his hair, and sat down at the table. Mama brought him a cup of coffee, and asked him if he would like a fried egg for breakfast.

He said, with much sarcasm, "Yes, of course. And throw in some chorizo and some potatoes, too." He knew there was neither in the house. We knew from the tone of his voice that this was no time to do or say anything that would call attention to ourselves, lest we become objects of his anger.

Mama brought his egg on a plate and placed it in front of him. Papa cut into the egg with the side of his fork. Then he stopped, stood up, and shouted, "This egg is not cooked properly!"

He threw the plate against the wall, where it broke into three pieces. The egg started running slowly down the side of the wall, with the yolk leaving some yellow streaks behind it. With that, he went out the door, slamming it behind him, and headed down the hill towards town.

After that outburst, not only Barbarita, but Mama and all us kids were crying. Mama picked up the largest piece of the broken plate, scraped what she could of the egg onto the plate, and took it into the kitchen. When she came back to us, she still had tears running down her cheeks.

She said, "Don't be afraid. Your father is very upset because his baby died, and because he is not working. But he loves you with all his heart. Things won't always be like this. Please finish your beans." But we all left the table, leaving our food on our plates, and for once we could truthfully say that we were not hungry.

The morning passed, and Mama became more frantic over Barbarita's crying, but she did not want us to see her so agitated, so she asked us to go outside and play. However, kids sense when something is wrong, and in times of trouble they want to be near their source of comfort. So in order to comply we would briefly go outside into the level spot behind our house, (you could scarcely call it a yard), throw some rocks down into the ditch, then go back inside the house.

Mama was trying everything she knew, everything she could, to get Barbarita to stop crying. However, nothing worked. Barbarita kept crying. Mama tried giving the baby Karo syrup, first full strength, then diluted. Then she would switch to Eagle condensed milk undiluted, but Barbarita was too weak to pull the milk through the nipple. Small portions in a spoon to the baby's mouth were also rejected. Mama tried warming the milk to body temperature and diluting it more, but nothing helped. Mama held Barbarita close, rocking her back and forth, crying softly herself. I heard her say, "If only your Aunt Cuca was pregnant again, and could come to breast feed you."

I heard her say several times with an air of desperation, "If only I had milk from my breast to give you. I'm so sorry. God forgive me." As if it were her fault.

My younger sister sneaked a spoonful of the Eagle milk, but Mama was too weak even to scold her.

Close to noon time, Mama called to Belia, "My daughter, I don't know what else to do. I have tried everything that I know, and I don't know what else I can do for the baby. She won't stop crying, she's very weak, and you are going to have to take her to the hospital for me. I'm not strong enough to take her. I hate to ask this of you, but I know you can do it. You know English well enough to tell the doctor what has been happening. Go right now! Put on your shoes and get her there as soon as you can!"

Belia took Barbarita in her arms and started walking to the hospital at the Little Daisy Mine, about a mile away, across town and downhill. The other hospital in town, the United Verde hospital, was practically next door, but they would not treat you unless you were a United Verde employee. So Belia crossed Giroux Street and took the zig-zag trail to Hill Street. She turned left, downhill, on Hill Street, past an older hospital that was now used as a clubhouse for United Verde employees. She continued to where Hill Street meets Clark Street near the Episcopal Church and continued down the stairs in front of the TF Miller store, that connects Clark Street to Main Street.

She turned left on Main Street to the end of the block, where she descended some rock steps to the Little Daisy Road. Little Daisy Road was an unpaved road that enclosed Mexican Town on both sides like a parabola. Mexican Town was an area of unpainted, weathered, wooden houses that balanced on long stilts supporting the downhill side of the houses.

From the bottom of the rock steps, Belia could see the hospital. The hospital had been built as a hotel for single, white professional employees who worked in the Little Daisy Mine. It was a beautiful building constructed of concrete, three stories high, with a facade of Spanish arches. When the Little Daisy started closing down, there was no more need to house professionals, but there were still some miners who needed care, so the hotel was converted into a hospital. In earlier, more prosperous times, the UVX corporation that owned the Little Daisy Mine had built a hospital for its miners on a hill to the southeast, across the canyon cut by Bitter Creek. When it became clear that prosperity would not last forever, UVX converted that completed hospital building into a school, and the site became known as Building C, a part of the complex that included the Jerome High School.

When Belia could see the hospital about a half-mile away, she gathered strength and quickened her steps. There were no other people on Daisy Road, so she started talking and singing over and over again to Barbarita.

"Ya no llores hermanita
Estamos pronto pa'llegar
Ya no llores mi bonita
El doctor te va aliviar.

En el hospital veras
Vas a ser bien recibida
Te daran la bienvenida
Ya no mas tu lloraras"

Don't cry more little sister
We will get there soon
Don't cry more my pretty
The doctor will make you well.

In the hospital you will see
You will be well received
They will welcome you
And you will cry no more.

When Belia's steps did not match the meter of her song, she skipped on one foot until she got back into the rhythm. Belia was so happy to think that her singing had soothed Barbarita, because the baby's crying had grown gradually softer. As Belia neared the hospital, the crying stopped altogether. They reached the hospital, and Belia walked through the main door.

Two nurses were at the reception counter that reached to Belia's shoulders. At a desk behind the counter, a young nurse was talking to an older nurse who was seated. The young nurse left the desk and approached Belia at the counter.

"What do you have there, my child. Can I help you? Do you speak English?"

"It's my little sister. Her name is Barbara."

"Let me see her. Can I hold her? What's wrong with her?"

"She's sick. She cries all the time, and she won't eat."

"Where is your mother? Why didn't she come?"

"My mother is sick, too, and she doesn't speak

English, so I had to bring her."

"Give me the baby. I'll take her," said the older nurse who had been sitting at the desk. She took the baby from the young nurse and said to her, "Edna, I'll handle this. This is the surviving twin of the one who died a month ago."

The older nurse unwrapped the baby, looked closely at her, held her up to her face, then wrapped her again and held her in her arms tenderly. The young nurse asked with a touch of urgency, "Shall I take her vitals? Shall I call the doctor?"

The older nurse gently handed the baby back to the young nurse, and said, "Do what you wish, Edna, but I think that if you check her first with the retinal sensitivity test, it will tell you everything you need to know."

The young nurse took the baby back to the examination table, took a penlight and directed the light into Barbarita's eyes. She looked up with a startled look and saw the older nurse shake her head and say quickly, "Don't say a word."

Turning to Belia, the older nurse said gently, "You can go home now. We will take care of your sister. And tell your father that he will have to come to the hospital in person, early tomorrow morning without fail. Do you understand that? Will you tell him that?"

Belia said, "Yes, ma'am," and started out the door.

Belia slowly retraced her steps towards home. She made slow progress, because it was uphill all the way. Frequently she stopped to rest and to cry. Her biggest worry was what to say to her mother. After some thought, she decided simply to tell her mother that the baby had something wrong with her eyes.

Epilogue

Barbarita was buried in a homemade wooden coffin lined with scraps of cloth taken from an old dress, next to her twin sister's grave. Both were buried in unmarked paupers' graves. The death certificates of the two infants listed the cause of death as malnutrition.

Father's Day

"May I interview your father now?" she asked in a voice as soft as a summer night.

"Why do you want to interview him? You know he's dying don't you?"

"Yes, I know. That's why I'm here. Please let me sit down, and I'll answer you. You're his son aren't you? May I call you Desi?"

"My name is Desiderio. I don't like Desi."

"I understand. My name is Elisa, Elisa Miranda, but I don't like being called Alice."

"That's fine Elisa. Do you speak Spanish?"

"*Si, como no.* Of course."

"That's good. He speaks pretty good English, but it's much less effort for him to speak in Spanish. Now tell me why you want to interview him."

"You know from my card that I am with the Oral History Department of the university. Your father worked in the mines of Jerome and there aren't many like him who are left. I am trying to record what it was like working in the mines in those times, what kind of men they were, what they did, how they lived."

"If you interview him, you will also learn how miners died, if they were lucky enough to have survived the accidents. He is dying of pneumonoconiosis."

"Is that contagious?"

"No. It's a lung disease miners get from breathing too much dust. You would have to spend a few years working underground with him, breathing the dust from the drilling machines, in order to get it. But there is no problem in just talking to him. I'm sure he will be glad, even proud, to tell you his story. He still has an ability to recall facts that will amaze you. His mind has always been that way, and he has not lost it yet. However, I am worried about his physical condition. He tires easily."

"Don't worry about that part. I have already checked with his doctor, and neither he nor I want to do anything to hurt him. The doctor is checking on him now, and I expect him to come out soon and tell me that it is okay for me to go ahead with the interview. And the doctor will check periodically to see that I have not overtired him."

"Does the university's clout extend even into this hospital?"

"This is our teaching hospital you know. So the answer is yes. But I want your permission, also, of course. Will you give me your consent to interview your father?"

"Si, como no."

"Let me start by asking you some questions to which you know the answers, and that will save some time. Is his name Leopoldo Rabago, born November 27, 1898, in Babiacora, Sonora, Mexico?"

"Yes, but he will tell you that he was born in 1900."

"Is he Indian? Is Babiacora a reservation?"

"No. He's Mexican, and Babiacora is just a small Mexican town about two hours south of Nogales. I think Babiacora comes from the Opata Indian language and means beautiful valley."

"Tell me first, Desiderio. Did you ever want to become a miner?"

"Very much so. I always looked up to him. Every boy wants to grow up to be like his father. I perhaps wanted it more than most boys. I would get up early to bring him back a doughnut from the Jerome Bakery that he would take with him to work, and then I would sit with him while he ate breakfast. I would be waiting for him every day to come home from work. I knew he was a miner, but I had no idea as a kid what that involved.
I used to worry more when he worked the night shift, thinking that he was unusually brave to work in the dark. After some time I realized that he always worked in the dark, that it is always dark in the mine!"

"Did he ever tell you that he wanted you to become a miner?"

"No, in fact I think that he wrote me off very early, when he concluded that I did not have the physical skills or the physical toughness or the mental toughness that it takes to be a miner."

"Why do you say that, and how early are we talking about?"

"Well, I can remember being about four years old. I had fallen down and had bruised and cut my knee. You know, just ordinary kid stuff. But it was bleeding, and I thought that all my blood would spill out and I would die. I ran to him and put my arms around his legs, expecting to be consoled in my dying moments. He looked at the abrasions and said simply, '*Los hombres no lloran* (Men don't cry),' and walked away. I was quite impressed by that I remember, and after a while

I went to him, told him I wanted to be like him, and asked him to teach me to be a miner. He said, 'Okay, let's start now.'

"Then he asked me to bring him two boards, and a hammer and a nail. He got on his knees and held the two boards together on the floor, and asked me to nail them to each other. I hit the nail on the head the first few tries, but then I missed the nail and hit his fingers. He did not get angry, instead he told me that the work of a miner requires unfailing attention, and letting one's mind wander from the task at hand was a sure way of getting killed in the mine. Looking back on my life, I can see that he was right, that I do not have what it takes to be a miner, because although I learned to concentrate better, I never got better at using my hands. I failed every wood-working and metal shop class that I was ever put into. To be a miner, you have to hit the nail on the head without any misses. After that one incident I never asked him again to teach me about becoming a miner."

I saw the doctor approaching behind Elisa, and he signaled that we could talk to his patient. Elisa Miranda asked me if I would like to accompany her, but I declined, telling her that she could get more information faster, if she went in alone.

Elisa Miranda walked down the hall, and entered a room that had a sign near the door, "No Smoking. Oxygen in Use." She was surprised to see such a pale, frail man in the bed, when she expected to see a larger, more muscular man.

She introduced herself, "Good morning, Mr. Rabago. I'm Elisa Miranda. Did anyone tell you why I am here to see you?"

"Yes, the doctor told me that you wanted to learn how to become a miner. Frankly, looking at you, I don't think you could ever make it."

Rare photograph of two miners working underground. The man on the right is the author's father, Leopoldo F. Rabago. The photo is displayed in the Jerome Historic State Park. Courtesy of Arizona State Parks.

Elisa laughed. "You're right, I wouldn't. Your son outside told me that you are a good judge of miner material, and that you told him a long time ago that he would not be a good miner."

She set her tape recorder on the low table and switched it on. "You don't mind if I record this, do you?"

"Go right ahead." He paused.

"Yes, I remember that day with my son. That was a long time ago. He was about four years old when I had him nail together the two end pieces of an orange crate. It was very soft wood, and I gave him a hammer with a short handle. He hit this finger on my left hand," and held up his ring finger.

"Your son has never forgotten that either. But why is such attention and concentration so necessary to a miner?"

"Let me tell you a story about that, and perhaps you will see why that is so."

"Please go ahead, and I will try not to interrupt."

"I was fifteen years old. I had already been working in the mines for two years."

"You started working in the mines when you were thirteen years old? I didn't think that was allowed by law. Is it?"

"You interrupted me, but that is okay. I started working in the mines at thirteen, but that was in Pilares, Mexico. The mine in Pilares was operated by the same people who ran the Little Daisy mine in Jerome. What I learned in Pilares is important, because it applies to mines everywhere."

"Please pardon my interruption, and continue with your story."

"As I was saying, I had been working already for two years, and I was working as a miner's helper. A miner's helper does many things, like bringing the steel, the drill bits, to the miner, bringing the dynamite, making a separate trip to bring the blasting caps. You do not want the dynamite and the blasting caps together until you're ready to blast, because that is too dangerous. You are also there because if an accident occurs, two men together are better than one man alone. That's probably why in Spanish mines, the helper is called a *compañero*, a companion.

"The helper performs a very important function when the miner is operating the drilling machine. The miner's helper keeps his hand on the drill and makes certain that the bit is tight in the machine, because you do not want the bit and the machine to become separated while the machine is operating. You will see why.

"On this day, it was a payday, the miner, Jesus Prado,

was operating the drilling machine. I had my hand on the bit. Maybe I should be more clear. When I say bit or drill, I am talking about a cylindrical piece of hardened steel about an inch in diameter, and more than six feet long. This drill is turned by the compressed air drilling machine, so that the drill bores a hole into the rock by a rotary pounding action. Those are the holes that are later filled with dynamite to blast apart the rock, but I am getting ahead of myself.

"Going back to when I told you that I had my hand on the drill, I felt the drill advance too far too quickly and I felt the speed of rotation shoot up. I instantly knew that the drill must be traversing a seam, a soft spot between two strata of hard rock. I knew also that when the drill hit the hard rock again, there would be trouble if we did not get the drill slowed down very quickly.

"I immediately screamed at Prado to stop the machine. I saw in his eyes that he must have been thinking of something else, and whatever he was thinking was his last thought on this earth. The drill had continued very rapidly through the soft strata that was not more than an inch or two wide, and then impacted violently against the hard rock on the other side. That broke the drill in a spiral fracture, and a part of that drill came flying out of the hole like a bullet, except that the bullet was two feet long. It hit Prado in the middle of his forehead and took out the top of his skull halfway back.

"That piece of steel continued spinning and clattering away from me. It splattered blood and brain matter across the roof, the walls and the floor of the drift until it finally came to rest. It was ugly, but I don't think that Prado felt a thing. I can't say for sure that he would have avoided the flying drill if he had been paying attention, but who knows, he might have been able to shut down the machine in time."

"My God! What did you do? You were just a kid! Were you scared? Did you cry? Did you quit the mine then?"

"I'll answer your questions in their order," he said, and then inhaled a deep breath of oxygen. "Of course I went for help, but I knew there was nothing they could do for him. I helped load his body onto the metal stretcher that is used for hauling out injured or dead miners. Poor man, I really liked him. He was a good man, but he was careless that time. Of course I was scared, because it is a frightening thing for death to strike out so close, and so suddenly. Nevertheless, a man has to learn to live with his fear and conquer it, or else he is no longer a man. No, I did not cry, because I had been taught that '*los hombres no lloran.*' And no, I did not quit the mine, since I was the support of my mother and younger brothers and sisters. The foreman let me go home early that day, because I went up to the surface with the body, and too much time would be lost before I could get back. But I was back to work the next morning, assigned to a different miner. I have never forgotten that accident. I learned a hard lesson that has served me well, because keeping my attention from wandering has probably saved me from danger more times than I am even aware of."

"I must say that you have made your point very well, Mr. Rabago," said Elisa, her voice shaking just a little bit. "Maybe you could proceed by telling me when you arrived in Jerome?"

The doctor looked into the room and asked, "Are you okay? Not too tired?"

"I'm fine. This lovely young woman is making me feel young again remembering my past," he said with a wink, and continued. "I arrived in Jerome on January 17, 1925, at three in the afternoon with a wife and a two-month-old daughter."

"What did you do first?"

"First I got us a place to stay for the night, and then we ate at the English Kitchen, a Chinese restaurant. We took the booth farthest from the door."

"What was Jerome like, then?"

"It was like all mining towns. But there was snow five feet deep on the ground, and it was very cold."

"What did you do next?"

" I left the family at the place I had rented, where I had told the landlord that I would pay by the night, but that soon I would pay him the rent for a month."

"Did you have a job waiting, or did you have a lot of money with you?"

"Neither. After we ate, and paid the night's rent, I had five dollars left in my pocket."

"So what did you do?"

"I went to the Copper Star restaurant on Main Street and got into a poker game."

"With your last five dollars?"

"Yes. I sat down to play. Ramiro was immediately on my left, then Juan Ayala, then Lencho Morales. Next to him was Damian, and on my right was Jose. I dealt the cards, and Juan opened for 25 cents. Lencho dropped out, and Damian called. Jose raised 25 cents, and I called the raise."

"Wait a minute. Are you describing a game that happened, let me see, fifty years ago?"

"Yes. You asked me to tell you what I did next, didn't you?"

"Well, yes. But I certainly didn't expect to get such details! Your memory is awesome."

"I suppose you're right. That must be why I was a good miner and gambler."

"Did you come out winner in that game?"

"Yes, but it took me three continuous days to win

enough money to pay the rent, to buy firewood, milk for the baby, and food for all of us."

"Mr. Rabago, your memory is God's gift to oral historians. After the poker game was over, did you start mining? How did a typical day go?"

"Sure. I will just give you the most important information. Let us say that I was working the day shift. I would get up, have breakfast, and walk to the mine. I would go to my locker in the change room and take off my street clothes. Then I hauled my work clothes down from the ceiling, where I had put them the day before to dry. You see, when we got off the work shift, we would take a shower in our work clothes to wash off the dirt and grime, then send the clothes by pulley up to the ceiling of the washroom to dry. After that, we would wash ourselves off and put on our street clothes to leave."

"Were the work clothes dry the next day?"

"Most of the time. Except in winter, when they were not always dry, but they were certainly always cold! After I was in my work clothes, I would take my hard hat and my lunch bucket, pick up my number, and get on the train that would take me into the main tunnel until we reached the cages that would take me down to my work."

"What was the number you picked up?" Elisa felt her heart pound. This was the kind of detailed information that was so hard to find in written histories – and the kind of information that could get her published at last. She listened intently.

"It was a round brass medallion with a number on it. Every miner always had an assigned number that was used to keep track of you. Mine was 507. When you finished your shift, you put the number back on the board. That way, the bosses knew that no one was left underground, perhaps injured or worse. If you neglected to put back your number, you would get fired for that."

"What did you feel when you were entering into the tunnel?"

"As if I were going down into my grave. It is not easy to look up into the blue sky, the sunshine, feel the fresh air, and wonder if this is the last time you will see them. You know that you are leaving those things to enter into a world where the sun never shines, where the air you breathe has to be pumped in, where there never seems to be enough of it. You go into a black world that will kill you with a misstep. It's a world that some miners believe is even beyond the realm of God. Does that answer your question?"

Elisa was silent for a moment, feeling the emotion behind his answer. "Yes, very well, thank you. What is that 'cage' that you talked about?"

"The cage was the elevator that took us down to where we worked. The cage was big. It was a double-decker that packed twenty men or more on each deck. First, the cage took me down to the 1000-foot level. From there I would walk to another shaft and another cage that took me down to the 4500-foot level. One minute I was at a mile-high elevation, then I was almost to sea level, all in a matter of minutes.

"When I arrived at my work station with my helper, we would get to work. My work station was where we had left off working at the end of the previous day. If the muckers had done their job, the rock that we had exploded would be cleared away and on its way to the smelter. The muckers would clear the tunnel with shovels, dump it into chutes, then dump the ore into cars. They are called cars, but they are really just heavy metal buckets that run on metal wheels. These cars are eventually formed into a train that runs on the haulage level, at the 1000-foot level. The train takes the ore outside to a bigger train that hauls it to the smelter.

"If the timberman has done his job, the drift has now been braced up with some strong 12x12 timbers. If that was done, the first thing I did was to inspect the roof for any loose rocks that might come down when the drilling machine starts its shaking and pounding. I had a ten-foot metal bar that I used to pry into any visible cracks, and I pounded on anything that looked like it might shake loose.

"If everything looked safe, then we were ready to start. We could see the tunnel's face, the hard rock that would be our day's work – to advance the drift by six more feet. Yes, advancing the drift by six feet was a day's work in my time. Before my time, when the mining was done by hand, a day's work for a miner was to advance the drift six inches per day. Before the mine closed in Jerome, there were ninety miles of tunnels, so you can see how much labor went into that accomplishment."

He paused and took another gulp of oxygen.

"The next step after checking for safety was to 'set up' the drilling machine, that is to secure it firmly between the floor and the roof of the drift. After that, we connected the compressed air to the drilling machine. The compressed air turned the drill, so that it drove the drill into the rock by a rotary and pounding action. After that, we connected the water line to the drilling machine.

"When I first started working in the mines, the drilling machines did not have a water connection. There was no water to cool the drill head, so we had to replace the drills much more frequently. But after the machines worked with water, we were constantly getting sprayed by the water spitting back from the drill holes, so our clothes were always wet, and frequently we were standing in water over our shoe tops. But it was worth it, because the water to the drill head kept down the dust from the pulverized rock. Unfortunately, I spent years breathing that dust. I don't believe that I would be in this hospital now if I had not breathed so much dust. My lungs show totally black on an x-ray plate, so when I first came in here, the doctors thought that I had a raging case of tuberculosis. They had me in isolation until they checked my old x-rays, and discovered that my lungs have been that way for years.

"Undoubtedly we should have worn respirators. We should have worn ear plugs too, because the noise from the drilling machine was horrendous. Imagine, Miss Miranda, if we were operating a jack hammer in a space about a quarter the size of this hospital room. In the mine, it would be worse than operating a jack hammer in here, because in the mine, the sound bounces off the hard walls of the drift."

"Didn't that affect your hearing?"

Mr. Rabago cupped his hand to his ear, and said, "Eh? What?" Then he laughed weakly, and said, "Relax, I'm just having some fun with you, Miss Miranda. Even with your soft voice I can still hear you well."

"Now back to my work, to what I did after I set up the machine, and was ready to start drilling. This is where my experience came in. I could look at the rock face, and I could pretty well gauge how many holes I would have to drill, usually somewhere between thirty-two and thirty-six holes. I knew where the holes should be located on the drift face, and what the spacing between the holes should be. An inexperienced miner would waste time unnecessarily drilling too many holes, or using a more powerful grade of dynamite than he needed, or using too many drills, and in the end not produce a nice rectangular shape in his work. That kind of knowledge cannot be taught out of a book.

It is only learned by working with an experienced miner before you start doing it by yourself. As I told you earlier, I started working in the mine at thirteen years old, and by the time that I turned seventeen I was already an experienced miner."

"What do you mean? Weren't you a miner when you started working in the mine?"

"In general terms you would be considered correct. But in mining terms, a miner is not just anyone who works in a mine. When you start working underground, you start off as a mucker, a laborer. A mucker does things like shoveling the waste into the mine cars, breaking rocks with a ten-pound hammer until they are small enough to pass through a grizzly, and other manual labor of that sort."

"I know what you mean," said Elisa eagerly. "I went to a Fourth of July celebration down in Bisbee, and I was most impressed by the mucking contest. Those men would pick up a shovel full of gravel on the ground, and then fling it through the air into the ore car. The remarkable thing was that the shape of the gravel flying through the air did not change after it left the shovel. It was still the same shape when it landed in the car. They were shoveling so fast that there was always a shovel full of dirt in the air! I couldn't believe it!"

"You are right. Every workman in a mine is very skilled at his job. A timberman, for example, works with very heavy 12x12 timbers, but his finished work looks like that of a cabinet maker, with one piece expertly dove-tailed into another. Except that a timberman, unlike a cabinet maker who builds a chair to support the weight of a human being, is building 'square sets' strong enough to support the weight of an entire mountain above him.

"In the same way, a miner is equally skilled at what he does. He is one who has mastered not only the art of proper drilling, as I have explained, but also the dangerous art of working with the dynamite that is used to explode the rock. Not every seventeen-year-old kid can be trusted with a box of dynamite! For that reason, I was proud of being a 'miner' at a young age."

The doctor peered in again, but the old miner ignored him and continued talking, and he went away.

"I generally did not have to drill more than thirty-six holes per day, but sometimes I was able to do the job with a smaller number of holes. The holes had to be drilled in a certain pattern, and at a certain angle. If the holes were drilled in the proper place at the proper angle, and thereafter exploded in the proper sequence, the face of the drift would be advanced six feet in the same rectangular shape, the same height and width of the existing drift.

"Proper spacing and proper angle meant that the drill holes near the 'roof,' the ceiling of the drift, were slanted slightly upwards at a shallow angle, and the holes near the bottom, the floor, were also directed downwards at a shallow angle. In the center, between the roof and the floor, some of the holes were spaced closer together and were slanted upwards; others were slanted downwards, both sets at steeper angles than the holes nearer the roof and the floor.

"Those holes near the center, between the floor and the roof, were the holes that did most of the major part of the breaking. In this part, both the horizontal and vertical separation of the holes, and the angles I used, depended upon my assessment of the hardness of the rock we were working with."

Elisa looked up from her notes and checked the tape. The old, frail man had come alive while telling his story. She was astonished at the detail he remembered.

"The next task was to fill the holes with dynamite, and prepare for blasting. I knew the proper grade of dynamite to use, because dynamite came in different grades of explosive power. I knew the proper number of sticks of dynamite to put into each hole.

"The next phase was very dangerous. I connected the dynamite sticks to the blasting caps. Blasting caps are used to produce a smaller explosion that sets off the bigger explosion of the dynamite. The blasting caps contain nitroglycerin, so they produce a good explosion all by themselves. The caps can explode if you drop them or jar them. Some old miners used to say that the blasting caps would explode if you did not talk to them gently and treat them with respect. So I was always respectful of them, especially when I connected the blasting caps to the dynamite. After that, I connected the cordite fuse and brought it out to the end of the hole. The last step was to fill the hole with wet earth, then very gently tamp the hole, taking extreme care not to explode the blasting caps. If the hole was properly tamped, the initial explosion of the blasting caps would also set off all the dynamite in the hole."

Elisa wiped a thin sheen of sweat from her forehead, looking a bit dazed. She'd had no idea mining was such intricate work.

"I know that everything that I have told you so far sounds complicated, but I hope that it will make sense to you when you listen to your tape. The next part is more complicated in a different way. The object is to fire, or explode, the holes in a particular sequence; you don't just set them all off all at the same time. It might sound as if there were only one explosion, but really there is an entire sequence of explosions. The holes near the middle fire first, and the holes near the roof and the floor fire last. Do you understand?"

Elisa nodded.

"The only way I had to control the sequence of the firing was to vary the length of the cordite fuse that went to each hole. These days, explosions can be controlled electrically to within thousands of a second. But we did all right in the old days with the methods that we had. I extended my drift with controlled explosions that advanced the face in a vertical plane. If the plane was too irregular, too jagged, it was a good indication that a hole had not fired, and there might be unexploded blasting caps and dynamite to blow a careless mucker to pieces. I never lost a mucker to carelessness.

"The last act of my work day was to light the cordite fuse. I would leave enough length of the fuse to give me and my helper time to get to a safe place, far enough away from the explosion and the carbon monoxide that it would release."

Elisa leaned forward intently. "How would you know how fast or how far the fuse had burned?"

"Good question. I would cut some v-shaped notches every few feet along the length of the fuse, and as the fire passed each notch, it would spit out flame and smoke. When I could see the fuse was burning properly, it was time to go. Oh, I forgot to tell you that we ate our lunch underground, too."

"What did your lunch consist of?"

"Usually two tacos of tortillas and beans. Sometimes a doughnut or an apple, and a thermos of coffee."

"That doesn't sound like enough nourishment for all the labor you have described."

"I guess it was adequate. Almost all of the miners from Mexico were like me, thin and wiry. I weighed 150 pounds. We weren't the big brawny miners that are pictured in the posters. Some of the Slavic men were bigger, and they probably ate more and weighed more. Still we were able to work those drilling machines that weighed as much as we did."

"I still think that you must have been undernourished. Besides the physical labor, you must have used up some energy in stressing out over the dangerous work you have described to me."

"You know what, Miss Miranda? I have not described the most dangerous work to you yet."

"You are kidding me, aren't you?"

"I'm afraid not. But if you have more time, I will tell you about it."

Elisa thought of the article she would write and the journal she would send it to, and smiled. "Please go ahead, Mr. Rabago."

"Everything that I have described to you involved drilling a horizontal drift. But how about doing the same thing straight up? That is called a raise, and it is used to connect one horizontal drift with another horizontal drift that is one hundred feet closer to the surface. And to put that more in your own frame of reference, one hundred feet is about the height of an eight-story building. So a raise is a 'tunnel,' you might say, going eight stories straight up! So of course if you are drilling straight up, anything that comes down will come straight down on your head, not in front of you!

"The part of the same technique that is used to drill a raise is used to follow a vertical ore body. You start from the bottom of the ore body, and work upwards. That is called 'stope' mining. The ore body is usually at an angle to the vertical, so you have to do a combination of vertical and lateral mining. Taking out the ore leaves a big void above you that is too dangerous to leave unsupported. In order to support it, you have to fill in with a lot of square sets to keep the stope from caving in. That's when you need a good timberman to work with you.

"Has anything that I have said made sense to you?"

"Oh yes, you are very clear in your descriptions. I have to say I'm extremely impressed by how technical your work was. When I get home, I will study the tape and my notes for the details. And you certainly have conveyed to me that mining was very dangerous work. I would never want to be a miner," she said, laughing a bit nervously. "But most of all, I now realize that a miner was no mere laborer. He was a very skilled workman."

"Thank you for grasping that, Miss Miranda. That is exactly what I was trying to convey to you. If you get nothing other than that from this conversation, I will still be very happy. I always felt that the work I did was worthwhile. You have lifted my spirits by listening to me, and letting me recall when I was young and strong. But I am old now, and I am getting very tired. Are we done for now? If we are not finished, maybe you can come back another time?"

He took several breaths of oxygen and was quiet.

Elisa quickly looked up from her notes. "Thank you Mr. Rabago for sharing your experiences with me. It's far more than I ever expected. I think that we are done, but let me see where we left off."

She was silent while she reviewed her notes, then she said with a slight laugh, "You know what? We stopped when you were down in the mine, after you had lit the fuse to ignite the charges. We hadn't gotten you out of the mine yet. But I don't want to tire you." She reached over to shut off the tape recorder. "I can come back."

Mr. Rabago put aside the oxygen mask. "We can't stop now. You can't leave me down there!" joked the old miner. He took another deep breath from his oxygen canister. "I can go on a bit more. I don't want you to leave me down there, even if it is only on the tape. But I will be brief. After we lit the main fuse and made certain that it was burning properly, my helper and I headed back to the closest shaft that would take us to the surface. We had to change cages, as we did on the way down. But finally, we would get up back up to the 500-foot level, and back out on the surface where the showers and the change room were located."

The man was quiet for a moment, resting. His eyes were fixed somewhere in the distance. Then, he continued, speaking slowly, "I would get out of the darkness and once more be grateful for the world of light and open air. It did not matter if the day was cloudy or windy, or if the air was cold, or if there was snow on the ground, it was still good to see the world outside, good to be back in God's world. My life was sometimes hard, but I always knew I could handle whatever happened, because nothing could be as bad as being stuck underground."

Elisa could see he was very tired. "Are you all right? We can stop whenever you want," she said.

"No, I want to finish," he said firmly. "I want you to know how the story ends. When I reached the change room, I put my metal tag back on the board. That was the precise moment that I could feel that another day underground was over and I had a great evening ahead of me. I would take off my shoes and walk into the shower room fully dressed in my work clothes. The water was cold, but it washed the dirt and dust and grime away. After I got my work clothes as clean as I could, I put them on a hanger and raised them to the roof on a pulley. Then I could put my street clothes back on and go out into the world above ground. And that was a typical day of a miner."

Elisa sat quietly. "I am so grateful to you for sharing this," she said. "Thank you."

"*De nada.* I really enjoyed your visit. Obviously, I still like to talk about mining, so you gave me another chance to talk about it. They used to say in Jerome that there was more mining done in the bars than there was underground! Thank you, Miss Miranda, it has been a pleasure. If my son is still out there would you ask him to come in?"

"I'll do that of course," she said as she rose out of her chair and extended her hand to the man lying in bed. He grasped it strongly and then let go.

"This interview with you has been one that I will never forget," said the oral historian. "I would never have gotten your insight into the life a miner anywhere else. I am glad that I can be a part of preserving a past that would have been lost otherwise. I assure you that the pleasure has all been mine. May I come back if I find there is something that I missed?"

"Most certainly, if I am still around. Come back whenever you wish." He closed his eyes and smiled.

When Miss Miranda reached the waiting room, the son did not immediately react to her approach. He seemed to be deep in thought. She touched his shoulder, and the touch startled him.

He said, "Oh, you're back! I was thinking about when I was a boy, and my father could scare me with a look, or a word. How is he now?"

"He was getting tired, but he wants to see you. It was a wonderful interview. He is an amazing man."

The son said simply, "I know." He then said good-bye to Miss Miranda, and headed back to his father's room. As he walked in, he said in a cordial voice, "Hi, Pop. Did you make a miner out of her?" He was looking for signs of fatigue. Miss Miranda had been with his father a long time. But he was surprised to see that his father seemed to want to keep talking.

"You know, son, before too long there probably will be women miners. But in my time, that never could have happened. You needed physical strength to handle the drilling machines. Some of them weighed more than I did, and very few women have that kind of strength. They are not designed for that. Another thing, you had to be brave to go into the mine. Women are brave in some ways that men can never be, but women place a different value on life, maybe because they are the ones that bring life into the world.

"And let's face it. Men are more risk takers, because that is something within us; maybe we are designed for that, or maybe it is just something that comes out in men when they are around other men. Working in a mine involves much risk taking, because too many things can go wrong unexpectedly. One rock alone, or an avalanche of rocks, can fall on your head, or the ground can drop out from under you, or the machine can come loose, wires and hoses can break, timbers can crack, you can trip while carrying blasting caps, your light can go out when you most need it, the ventilation system can break down, I could go on and on, but you get the idea."

"Oh I get the idea, Pop. I was the one who couldn't make the grade as a miner, remember?"

"Well, you were good at what you did," said his father. He looked out the hospital room window, as though he were looking into another world. "Another thing that is so different now is that in my time, women did not work, only men worked. That meant that my wife, my children, you, depended upon me making that effort. That is a very strong obligation and incentive. I guess you could call it a man's sacrifice to do a man's work in the mine every day. I did it for you, and I have no regrets."

He sighed deeply. "Although it is true that I could

have done a better job of raising my children, but you have all done well, so maybe that is all I can ask for.

"Look at you, you have come to visit me straight from your work, and you are dressed in a suit and tie! I once dreamed of being able to do that myself, but it was not to be. Seeing you do your work dressed like that is enough for me. Maybe all my lectures and discipline that was perhaps sometimes too harsh did some good. I must have taught you something right!"

"You taught me more than you know. You were teaching me from the time that I can remember. I used to listen to you and my uncles Francisco and Alejandro talking mining talk to each other. I didn't understand it then, but I didn't forget it. Of course I wanted to grow up to be a miner, a man just like you. But you know what, Dad, until I overheard you explaining your work to Elisa Miranda, I did not realize how difficult and complex and demanding your work really was. Maybe if I had known this all along, you and I would not have had so many differences."

His father smiled a bit wearily. "Don't worry about it, son. That's the way life is, and what is done is done. I knew that you would never be a miner, so I let you go your own way. It was hard putting up with you sometimes because you were such a smart-ass. We were just born different, that's all."

"I hope that we are not too different. You see, I am still trying to be the man you have been all your life. How can I thank you for the example you have given me?"

"Why don't you tell your children what a miner was and what he did? Be sure to tell them that a miner was a man, *un hombre muy hombre*. That way I will not be forgotten. That is all the thanks I need, and it's something that I can take with me."

Desiderio reached out and took his father's hand.

Miss Daisy's Boudoir

"**M**y superintendent is walking like an old man!" thought James Douglas as he watched George Kingdon leave his house and start walking towards the mine. The superintendent's clothing was the same as always, a short-sleeved khaki shirt that showed muscular arms and shoulders, even under the shirt. His khaki pants were baggy as usual. George Kingdon was wearing his miner's hard hat, a carbide lamp attached in front, so it was obvious that he was headed for the mine.

"I know that man so well that I expect him to stop about now and light a cigar." As expected, George took a cigar out of his left shirt pocket and bit off the end. He lit a match that flared yellow at first in the clear morning air of Jerome, then settled into a blue flame that George applied to the end of the cigar. Douglas could see the white smoke of the first few quick puffs on the cigar, and he imagined that he could almost smell its burning aroma, even from behind the window where he stood watching.

Normally, George had the self-assured walk of a man who had been among hard men all his life, like a gunfighter who had learned some time ago that he would meet no real challengers. But Douglas knew the reason for the defeated walk this morning, and also knew that George would call on him in about an hour, after he had checked with the shift boss and made certain that the work in the mine was progressing normally.

After one hour had passed, right on schedule, Douglas heard his doorbell ring. He opened the door and said, with a smile in his voice, "Top of the morning to you, George!"

"Top of the slag dump to you too, Jimmy."

"Things aren't that bad, are they?"

"Hell, Jimmy. I know you well enough to know that you haven't called me over this morning to tell me what a good job I'm doing."

"Come on in and let's talk about it. We'll sit out on the veranda so that you can finish smoking your cigar."

"Are things that bad? If you offer me a brandy now, I will know that I really am in trouble."

"That is not a bad idea. I have some good Napoleon cognac that I have been waiting to try. We might as well enjoy these things while we can."

They sat on the veranda, and after Jimmy had poured the cognac, he asked, "How are things below?"

"Great! Everyone is working like a slave. It reminds me of the inside of an ant hill, which reminds me of something else. Jimmy, if we don't find any precious metals in this mine, we can cut a vertical section through the mine, then cover it with a big piece of glass, and charge admission to see all the miners scurrying about underground! What do you think of the idea?"

"Stop joking, George. We have work to do this morning. But speaking of precious metals, I can't say that I've seen much of that stuff in all these years that we've been looking here. How long has it been? You know, I went to the dentist last week, and I didn't have enough gold on me to fill one of my teeth. It wasn't that big a filling either. If that didn't make me feel humble! Maybe my superintendent has been taking it all?"

"I didn't think that you had noticed, Jimmy. I will have to admit that I was taking it, but I stopped about a week ago. Before that, I was stuffing my pockets every night. But with copper at only 13 cents a pound, I could not steal enough to pay for the pants whose pockets I was ripping out."

"That must be why I saw you walking this morning like an old man, looking so tired out. You must have tired yourself out carrying all that copper. Copper ore gets heavy."

"Give me another shot of brandy, and let's get down to business."

"I agree," Jimmy said, as he unrolled the drawings of the underground mine workings.

"Don't spill any cognac on these, as they may be in a museum someday as the most expensive drawings in history. What do you say we go over things from the beginning? Stop me if you see where there might be some mistake in my logic. Maybe we can determine where we might have gone wrong.

"First of all," continued Douglas. "I don't think that we are wrong in our basic assumption that Old Mother Earth must have sheared off the top of the United Verde ore body that is uphill from us, over on the west side of the Verde Fault. Outcroppings as broad as they found over there are rare. The topmost part of the ore body must have sheared off, and it had to go downhill, to this side of the Verde Fault, where we have been working. And let's see, we had to go through 500 feet of overburden. That is what we have done so far, isn't it?"

His superintendent replied, "That is true, but that man Fisher, that surveyor, did a lot of our work for us. He was amazing. First he found that little triangle of unclaimed land next to the big March Claim, so he claimed it for himself and called it the Little Daisy Claim. Nothing too unusual there, but it was unusual to build a Chinese laundry over his claim, so that he could work his claim underneath it.

"I guess he figured that the Chinese were the only ones who would not be able to tell anyone what he was doing. He must have dug the shaft a bucket full at a time."

"Correct, George," said Douglas. "But Fisher was lucky that he was digging right alongside the Verde Fault where the earth was soft, otherwise he never would have been able to do what he did. He put himself in terrible danger of a cave-in, though. At least he did get some money when he sold us his claim. He not only gave us a name, The Little Daisy, but we only had to extend his shaft a 100 feet deeper to realize that the ore body we were looking for was not up against the Verde Fault. From all that, we have to assume that the ore body that we are looking for has to be deeper and farther east, farther downhill from the fault."

The superintendent took a sip of his cognac, then spoke, "I agree with you so far, Jimmy. But knowing that the ore body has to be deeper and farther downhill doesn't tell us much, does it? It could have traveled all the way down to Clarkdale or across the Verde River, for all we know. Maybe we overpaid him for his claim?"

"Now, George. Give the man some credit. He sold us the claim just at the right time, just when he had dug deep enough to show that his claim had promise, but not so far that he dug past the promising deposits. He not only knew what he was doing, he was also lucky and audacious."

Douglas was silent for a moment before he said, almost as if speaking to himself, "Maybe that is the kind of man that we need now."

"Do you mean an audacious man, not a plodding and methodical man like me? Is that what you want to tell me? Jimmy, are you going to can me?"

"Now, George, you know that I won't do that, and that is not why I wanted to meet with you. You have been with me ever since Pilares. You are the one person with whom I can be completely honest. We have made a lot of decisions together and most of them have been right. But I have to admit that I have run out my lucky streak on this mine. I'm afraid that I have to can myself, and if I go, everyone else goes with me."

"You're not giving up now, are you? What brings this on?"

"George, I've never held anything back from you, and I am not going to start doing that now. But the problem is that I have had $250,000 of my investors' money for two years now, money that was specifically to be used for the development of this mine. We started using that money more than two years ago, when we first started to sink the Edith shaft. And how deep are we now?"

"At the 1400-foot level."

"But we haven't found anything worthwhile, have we?"

"That is true. But we have found just enough to make me want to keep going."

"With all my being, George, I too want to keep going. But you need to know that we have used up all the exploration money without finding anything. There isn't any more money. Now I have to tell our investors that we have nothing to return to them, that there will be no dividends. I have to tell them that we have failed."

Jimmy Douglas shook his head and said, "What makes me feel especially bad is that I solicited this money on my good name. That money did not come from just the general public. It came from metallurgists, geologists, mining engineers, all people like that, people in our business. They invested in this venture because of our past successes. That is why I feel that my personal reputation is on the line, and I find it hard to admit to myself that I have let them down.

"The last straw was the report I got from the geologist that I imported from that fancy school of mines back East. I received it a few days ago, but I wanted to think things over before I talked to you. He has looked over all our drawings, every assay report, every core sample. He has walked every drift on every level in the mine. Based on all that, his recommendation is that we close up shop, that we cut our losses, because he sees nothing in what we have shown him that could justify spending any more money. He says that there's nothing here of value to be found. With that kind of report from the learned doctor professor, how could I live with myself if I spent more money of my investor friends, even if I had any money left to spend?"

"As Cornish miners say..."

"George, I know, I know. I've heard that Cornish saying a thousand times. 'Never quit drilling until you have fired another round.' I also know what the Welsh miners say, 'Pay dirt is always four feet from where you stopped working.' Sometimes I wish that our work was as simple or as impossible as that. But George, I have to be realistic. I have been working with other people's money, and I don't have anything to give back to them. That is what makes my decision so difficult for me now."

Jimmy Douglas took a sip of his drink and looked into the distance. "There is something else that makes this so difficult. I have lived in many mining towns, but Jerome is special to me, in ways that I don't really understand and can't explain. Why I have even started sketching plans for a big home that I would like to build where we are now sitting. I want to put in a wine cellar, a smoking room, a pool table, and a porch with a wide overhang where I could sit and contemplate the view. I could put in a school where the miners could educate their children. And now I am afraid that none of those dreams will ever come true."

"Jimmy, are you telling me that you have decided to shut this mine down, to give up and run off to Chile or somewhere, with your tail between your legs?"

"Don't make things harder for me, George." He started rolling up the drawings. "Start shutting down this operation."

"When, tomorrow? At the end of the shift today?"

"Nothing that sudden. But you can start laying off the men one or two at a time, starting with your least productive men and saving your best men to the last."

"That means we will have a crew of Mexican miners pretty soon."

"That's all right, I don't care what they say up at the Big Mine. But we must start to close things down right away."

The superintendent looked his boss in the eye. "It sounds as if you've made up your mind, and I respect your decision. How much time do I have before I kick the last man out and put a lock on the Edith Shaft?"

"First let me ask you something. I have been discussing this situation with my friend Tener, and I have been completely honest with him about the outside evaluation and everything else. He has been with us from the start, remember we even named the Edith Shaft after his daughter. After having come this far, he is willing to help us to shut down in an orderly way. He and I have talked about putting up $25,000 to do that. He is willing to put up half of that. If I put up the other half, how much more time would $25,000 buy us?"

"We could make it to the end of the year, having laid off half of the men."

"That is about what I had hoped that you would say, and it is about what I had calculated. Since that is personal money and not investors' money, I can use it in good conscience. So you have until the end of December to shut things down."

"Do you have any specific instructions as to what you want us to do in the time we have left?"

"George, I will leave that to your best judgment. But I'm feeling that maybe we've been thinking and acting too much like geologists and mining engineers. If logical thinking was all it took to find this elusive ore body, we should have found it a year ago. Maybe we should start thinking about this ore body as we think of a beautiful woman we are pursuing. A woman who has been tantalizing us by leaving a handkerchief here, a scent of her perfume there, letting us have an occasional warm touch, just to make herself more alluring when we do finally catch up to her in her boudoir. Do you follow me?"

George leapt to his feet. "Hell no, Jimmy! I think your desperation has gotten the better of you! Damn it man, I have my own reputation to consider! What do you think would happen if I told my crews that we're supposed to be looking for the scent of perfume down there? Do you think anyone would follow my orders? They would think that maybe I had been breathing too much carbon monoxide. Hell, Jimmy, maybe we should shut down right now, while both of our reputations are still more or less intact. After all, it's not every mine that pays off!"

"Calm down, George. Sit down. What I'm trying to tell you is that we have to become more lucky and audacious. Forget what I said about perfume. But we are truly desperate, and there is no money left to just go on doing what we have been doing."

George sat down. "At least help me out a little bit! What the hell is a 'boo-dore' anyway?"

"It's French for a woman's private room. It's pronounced 'boo-dwahr,' George. Let's just continue to the end of the year the best we can. But I don't want you to give lay off notices to your last crew until after Christmas. And don't hire any new men."

"Well, you're a little late for that, Jimmy. I hired a new man yesterday to replace the one who lost his leg last week. This new man said that he worked for us down in Pilares, and he's a good miner."

"What's his name?"

"Jeremiah Sanchez."

"Jeremiah was a biblical prophet and we could sure use one. Maybe that is a good omen. But he is absolutely the last hire."

"Jimmy, I'm not leaving until you tell me where I am to search for Miss Daisy's boo-dor, or whatever you call it."

"It's bood-wahr, George."

"Okay, but where do I look for whatever you call it? We are already down to 1400 feet. We can go a little deeper. Do you want me to do that?"

"No, my feeling is that we should backtrack a little, to see if we can pick up Miss Daisy's trail. Go back to the 1200-level and look for her upwards, downwards and sideways."

"I got it, Jimmy. Now if you'll excuse me, I think

were done. I've got a woman to chase after, and I'm not talking about my wife."

Several weeks passed, and in the first week of December the superintendent was making his rounds underground. At the 1200-foot level, he noticed something unusual that caught his eye. There was a stope, a cavern-like room, that had followed a small but nearly vertical ore body. The drift had been widened to three times its normal width near the stope, and the roof over the stope had been extended thirty feet above the floor. That was where the ore body had ended. This was just another one of those small ore bodies that had caused such initial excitement, and had raised hopes that a significant ore body had been found. But like many others, it had ended in disappointment.

"This is another of those 'handkerchiefs' that the boss was talking about," the superintendent thought to himself.

But there was something unusual about the wooden platform that had been laid down over the waste used to fill the stope. The wooden platform had been used to start a cross-cut at right angles to the drift, twenty-four feet higher than the 1200-foot level.

"That's quite unusual," the superintendent noted. "Why would anyone start a cross-cut from a worked-out stope?"

He climbed onto the wooden platform and directed his light into the cross-cut that was only about thirty feet deep. "About five days work to drill that far," he reasoned. The shape of the new drift was almost perfectly rectangular and the walls were comparatively smooth. "The work of a good miner," he observed.

Nobody was working the stope. When the superintendent met the foreman a little later, he asked him, "Who was working the cross-cut off the old stope?"

"That new guy, Jeremiah," came the reply.

"Where is Jeremiah now?"

"He was pulled off by the mining engineer."

The superintendent concluded that the mining engineer must have a reason for doing the cross-cut, and decided that the next time he saw the engineer, he would ask him about it.

At the end of the shift on December 20th, 1914, George left early for his home that was near the mine. The thought that he would soon have to give the final lay-off notices to the remaining workers was weighing heavily on him. When he had almost reached the front door of his house, he heard and saw someone running from the mine towards him. He recognized the shift boss and surmised that there must be some trouble, so he started walking back towards the man.

The shift boss was out of breath so it took him a moment to recover and say, "George, I may have big trouble, or maybe it is nothing. Hurry back with me and I'll tell you on the way."

"Okay, but before we get there, I want to know the entire problem."

"The problem is that we may have a man under-ground on the 1200-foot level that I can't account for!"

"What do you mean 'may have?' Do you or don't you have a man unaccounted for?"

"That's the problem. I don't know! The numbered tags are all back on the board. That tells me that everyone is out of the mine."

"Isn't that good enough for you?"

"The problem isn't that simple, George. There is an incredible story that is hard to ignore, because it comes from one of my most reliable men, Victor Sanchez."

"Isn't Victor one of the miners who came with us from Pilares?"

"Yes, that's correct. Victor is the man who was

buried for two days in a cave-in, before we got him out alive."

"Yes, I remember that incident. Wasn't there someone else killed alongside him, or something like that?"

"Yes, his partner."

"Well why are we wasting so much time standing here talking if there is a man missing underground? We must go down and look, instead of talking about an old accident."

"Hang on, George. Our present problem and that old accident are all related, I am told."

"Damn it, man, what is the relationship? Sullivan, you had better make a damn good explanation, and do it fast!"

"Victor Sanchez says that when he was buried in that cave-in, his partner had been buried above and behind him. As soon as we uncovered Victor's face and he was able to speak, he told us to hurry and free his partner, that his partner was alive, and had been urging him to hold on, not to give up, not to lose hope. Victor said the partner had been talking to him the whole time they were buried, and had been talking to him right up to the time we uncovered Victor's face. But when we uncovered the partner two hours later, it was obvious that the man had been killed instantly in the cave-in, so he could not possibly have been talking to Victor."

"Sullivan, get to the point. What the hell does that all that have to do with this present problem?"

"I'm almost there. Victor tells me that at the end of his shift today, he was coming up in the cage from the 1400-foot level. When the cage reached the 1200-foot level, it didn't make a stop because all the men had supposedly been cleared from that level. But Victor swears that there was a man standing there, and as

Victor's light swept past the man's face, he recognized the face of his dead partner! I know this sounds pretty incredible. If this story had come from anyone other than Victor, I would not even have bothered you."

"Tell me what you have done thus far to resolve this."

"I made a head count of all the men who were working underground on that shift. They are all on the surface and accounted for, except for the new man, Jeremiah."

"Is his number on the board?

"Yes."

"Did anyone else hang up his number?"

"No. At least no one admits doing that, and I believe them. They know that is cause for immediate termination."

"Then we have to go down and search for the man ourselves. Call Victor."

"He refuses to go back down."

"Then we will have to go without him. Get six other men, and we'll start at the 1400-foot level, and search upwards until we find him."

The superintendent, the shift boss and the other men reached the 1400-foot level, the lowest level of the mine. As they exited the cage to start searching the different drifts, they heard an explosion come from higher up the shaft. They froze, listening for rocks or timbers to come falling down. If anything came down, the men knew that they would be trapped. After a short time had passed and nothing fell from above, the superintendent ordered, "All get back in the cage. Sullivan, ring the bell for an emergency lift!"

As the cage neared the 1200-foot level, George smelled the sweet scent of exploded dynamite. He rang the bell for a stop, and said, "We'll search at this level to find out where that explosion came from!"

The superintendent himself led the way, following the scent, until he came to the wide spot in the drift where the dust of the explosion floated in the air. It was coming from that unusual cross-cut. He climbed up to the wooden platform where the strange cross-cut started, and directed the light on his helmet into the dust, but he could not see more than five feet ahead.

He proceeded farther into the cross-cut, very carefully checking his every step, to be certain that he did not step on a body. He arrived at the place where the rocks had been blown back by the explosion, and reasoned that if a man had been in the cross-cut, his body would also have been blown back by the same explosion. He checked over the rocks carefully, looking down to see if there was any sign of a man buried underneath them. He kept going, without seeing any body or parts of a body, until he reached the end of the cross-cut.

When his light illuminated the face of the drift, he was absolutely stunned. Never before in all his mining experience had he ever seen anything like it. He was looking at a vein of copper ore that was as wide as the drift, and looked like it extended above, below, and beyond the side walls. He could see the streaks of native copper through the ore, so he knew this vein was richer than anything he had ever believed possible. He took out his knife and dug out a length of native copper. Only then did he believe his eyes.

The men behind him could hear the excitement in his voice when he yelled out, "This is the boo-dor! We have found Miss Daisy's boo-dor!" The men thought that the superintendent had lost his mind. Then they too saw the strike and started their own celebration.

The search for Jeremiah was forgotten momentarily

in all the excitement. George was the first to recover, and knew immediately that he would not have to limit his costs, or give any lay-off notices. He ordered a full search of the entire mine at the overtime rate of pay. No body was ever found. The following day was a payday. Jeremiah did not show up to claim his pay check.

After the search was over, the superintendent immediately went to tell Jimmy Douglas the news of the fantastic find. Douglas' face radiated relief and gratitude, but the dominant emotion on his face was an expression of awe and wonder. Douglas lapsed into a deep silence. When he recovered he asked, "George, did we take good care of the widow and family of the man who was killed in the cave-in at Pilares with Victor?"

"Yes, I would say that you were more than generous."

"Thank heaven for that, George. But can you tell me what you think really happened here?"

"I can't even pretend to know, and I am not even sure that I want to know. Victor has not changed his story. He still swears by it. Whatever the truth is, some good miner drilled that cross-cut. The mining engineer said that he did not order that cross-cut, that it was not his idea."

"I don't suppose we will ever know how it happened. But the bonanza is real enough, and I guess that we will just have to live with it, right? May I offer you another cognac by way of celebration, George?"

The two men clinked their glasses and their eyes met. "To Miss Daisy's boudoir," said Jimmy Douglas.

Headless Charlie

Bobby stood staring scared and dumbfounded, as he watched the planchette of the Ouija board move from one letter to the next spelling out: U-R-N-D-A-N-G-E-R. His knees went weak, he felt faint, and a chill came over him. His stomach turned over uneasily. He hoped that he had not wet his pants.

What had frightened him was the fact that the planchette was moving all by itself! He was the closest person to the Ouija board on the library table, and he was more than ten feet away from it! The only other person in the library was the librarian, who was looking at the shelf of books behind her, so she had not seen what was happening.

"What is going on here?" he thought to himself. "What I see makes our theory stupid and ridiculous!"

Bobby had come to the library expecting to meet his friend David, with whom he was working on a project for their high school science class. The subject they had chosen was "The Ouija Board." They wanted to show that there was nothing mysterious about the board, and planned to prove that the planchette was really moved by the conscious or unconscious muscle movements of the players and that there was nothing occult about it. But Bobby could not explain what he was seeing – that without a human touch, that planchette was moving of its own volition!

As Bobby struggled to find an explanation, he heard David walk into the library. Bobby hesitated, wondering how to tell David that the planchette had moved by itself, without showing his fear or without appearing ridiculous.

David, however, did not give Bobby a chance to speak. David said, "This is what I've learned so far," and handed him a sheet of paper. "I cannot stay, my grandmother is waiting outside for me," and he started out the door.

Bobby followed David outside where he stood next to his grandmother and told him, "I don't want to play with the Ouija board. You will have to work it all by yourself!"

"Why not? Are you scared?"

"Of course not," Bobby lied. He blurted out the first reason that he could think of, "It's because the Catholic Church forbids it. The church says that the Ouija board is a way of communicating with demons!"

David's grandmother interjected, "You Catholics are strange. This is the 20th century and that kind of thinking died out centuries ago. Come, David, we have to go."

David responded, "I don't mind doing it myself, but I think that it will be harder to prove our theory with just one operator. Let's talk about it this weekend, okay?"

Bobby walked back to the library. He wondered whether he should ask permission to stay from the librarian. After all, he was a "Mexican," and he was no longer in the company of one of his "American" friends. Bobby knew the unspoken rule in Jerome that Mexicans were not welcome in the town library. He looked at the librarian who seemed unconcerned and who continued her work on the shelf.

He sat down at a table next to the one with the Ouija board. His mind was flooded with questions. "Am I moving it with my mind? Is something trying to tell me something? Who or what is it? What is the danger to me? What am I afraid of ? What is there to be afraid of?"

Bobby forced himself to get up and walk to the table with the Ouija board. He put his shaking hands on the planchette, and consciously moved it to spell out the question, "Are you a demon?"

His fingers almost slipped off the planchette when it moved quickly and forcefully to the corner of the board that read "no." He was very relieved that it had not gone to the corner that read "yes."

Then Bobby spelled out, letter by letter, "What do you want?"

Letter by letter, the board spelled out, "Talk."

In the same way, Bobby spelled out, "Go ahead."

The board answered, "2maro. clark st schl. 8pm."

The following evening at 7:00 pm, Bobby started watching the Clark Street School grounds from his house, which was very near. He saw no one enter or leave the grounds, so at 7:45 he walked onto the upper playground. It was getting dark, but there was still light enough to see clearly. He could see no one.

Bobby had come by himself, still afraid, but also afraid to tell anyone why he was there. He did not know what to expect, but he was afraid that he might see flying Ouija boards, hear the sounds of rattling bones and dragging chains, perhaps see figures in white sheets flying all over the place, but he saw nothing.

He sat on the bottom step on one of the porticos. The portico had a square pillar at each corner, flanked by a Doric column on each side of the pillar. As he sat watching for someone to enter the playground, he was startled to hear a voice from behind the Doric column. It was a young man's voice, in a tone that sounded perfectly normal and human, with the slight accent of a person who had spoken Spanish before learning English. The voice startled him, for he was sure that no one had been in that portico when he arrived; he had seen no one come into the playground, and had not heard any opening of the heavy copper doors behind him. The sound caused the hair on the back of his neck to stiffen, he got goose-bumps, and a chill went through him.

"Thank you for coming," the voice said. "But don't look back at me. I don't want to scare you."

"I thought you said you weren't a demon!"

"I am not. I'm just a normal person, or more correctly, a normal ghost of a normal person, except that I have part of me missing. That might scare you if you looked at me."

"Christ, I don't think that you could scare me anymore than I am right now! I am sorry that I came! I'm leaving! I don't want anything to do with you!"

The voice softened into a more pleading tone. "Listen, I'm not trying to harm you; on the contrary, I am trying to help you! I want you to listen to me, because you are in very serious danger and you don't even know it! I want to save you if I can."

"Why are you bothering with me? Don't you have other people to help?"

"If we can continue to talk, it will be clear why I have chosen you. We have to do it this way or not at all. Ouija boards are just too slow, and you may not have much time left. But if you really want to go, go now, and you will never see me or hear from me again. What do you want to do?"

"Am I really in danger?"

"Yes, very much so!"

"Are you the Devil?"

"Of course not! Perhaps I can convince you in this way. Do you know the saying, 'Tell me who your friends are and I will tell you who you are?' "

"Yes, my mother has said that to me many times."

"Well, I propose that if you want my help and want to meet again, I will bring some of my friends to talk with you, and maybe you may be more willing to accept my help. You will be able to see them and talk to them without being frightened too much. One of them has some parts missing too, but he is not as deformed as I. Perhaps you may even know him. I know you will remember a woman that I will also bring. If you can accept them, perhaps you will accept me too, or at least accept my help. What do you say?"

"I am willing to go ahead."

"Good. Then come here again tomorrow. But be here at 8:30, when it's a little darker. Again I warn you not to look back tonight. My friends will also come out from behind here. They will walk out in front of you, where you will be able to see them and talk to them. But don't try to touch them or hold them. Agreed?"

After Bobby had agreed, he sat still for a few minutes until he was certain that whatever belonged to the voice was gone. Then he stepped around the column into the portico behind him. He was not surprised to see nobody there.

The next evening, he was there at the appointed time and heard the same voice say, "Thank you for coming, Bobby. I hope that you are not as afraid as you were yesterday evening."

"How do you know my name?"

"You will be surprised at how much I know about you. However, I can't explain everything to you right now. It is not your time yet to know how things work on this other side."

"What is that 'other side?' "

"Look, let's not get sidetracked. We have no time to waste. Better let me show you what I have prepared for you, and maybe we will have some time later for your questions. Is that all right?"

"I'm sorry, please go ahead."

Immediately a woman's figure came out from the portico behind him. He saw a thin woman, wearing a faded blue dress that looked home made. The dress reached half-way to her ankles, and below the hem of her dress he could see tan cotton stockings that older women wore a long time ago. He could see her very clearly, as clearly as he had seen his own brothers and sisters just a short time before. The woman gave no appearance of being ghostly, or ephemeral or apparitional. The only thing different was that she seemed to glide rather than to walk, and that her shoes made no noise on the gravel of the school playground. As she turned around to face him, he noted that she had straight black hair streaked with gray. He recognized the delicate features of her nose and cheeks, then he noted the soft kind eyes, and the thin lips that were smiling at him.

"Nana Carolina!" he managed to say."

"Yes, *mi hijo.* It is I, your grandmother. Your friend here asked me to come, so of course I could not pass up the chance to help him, to help you, and to see you and talk to you."

"Nana, it's been almost fifteen years since we last talked. I remember that I was crying because a bee had stung me on my toe. You put mud on it, and that took away the pain and I stopped crying. But I don't remember that I ever thanked you."

"You did thank me. I remember that bee sting well."

"Nana, I remember that you died not long after that. I remember when they buried you. They lowered your coffin into the grave with ropes, and when they started shoveling dirt on top of your coffin, everyone there started to cry. I had never seen grown-ups cry before, but all your sons and daughters were crying. Even my father was crying."

"I was crying too, but no one could see or hear me anymore."

"Everyone grieved your death for a long time. My Uncle Francisco even became an alcoholic after you died."

"Yes I know. He was my youngest boy and we were very close. But I know that he is going to get over it."

"He blamed himself for your death because he signed the consent for your operation. I suppose he reasoned that if he had not signed the consent, you would not have died."

"Don't tell him that you talked to me and I told you that he was not responsible for my death. If you tell him that we talked tonight, he won't believe you and he will think you're crazy. But let me tell you what really happened, and little by little you can persuade him that he was not to blame. Please do this for me."

"Of course I will, Nana. All I know is that you died of pneumonia."

"I will tell you what happened. I went into the hospital for appendicitis. The operation went well but it was in recuperation that my problems started. At first I could get around by myself, but I kept getting weaker. For a time, the nurses helped me to get out of bed, but I think they got tired of doing so. They told me that they had more important matters to take care of, maybe they meant the miners who could be sent back to work were more important than old ladies like me. After that, they put me in that room where they put people to die. I could not get up by myself anymore, so of course I quickly got pneumonia and died from it. So you see that it wasn't really the operation that caused my death. I want you to convince Francisco of that, but do it carefully. You won't forget, will you? Now I'm sorry, but I must go."

"Please don't go, Nana, I hardly got to know you when you were alive, and I want to talk to you some more!"

"I know, my son. But I can't stay any longer with you. We will meet again, I can assure you of that." Then she went back into the portico and I heard her no more.

After that, the young man's voice, now familiar to me, said "Well, what do you think now? Do you trust me more and would like to go on?"

"Certainly. If my grandmother came with you, then you must be someone or something good. Please show me all you can."

Next a man glided out who looked to be about thirty years old, dressed in dusty gray denim pants and jacket. The skin of his face and arms looked like leather, like those of a man who has spent a lot of time out in the sun, or in front of hot flames. Bobby worked up enough nerve to ask him, "Are you from hell?"

The man laughed a hearty laugh that showed beautiful white teeth contrasting with his brown skin. He said, "No, I'm not from that hell that you're thinking of. I came from a different kind of hell. Maybe you've heard of me? I'm Juan de la Cruz."

"No, I'm afraid that I don't know you."

"I am also known as 'Juan of the Slag Pots.'"

"You're Juan? My English teacher recites a poem by that name. I can't believe that you are really him!"

Then Juan made a face at me, turned down the corners of his mouth and made his facial features hard. He slumped his shoulders. "Now, don't I look sullen and grim, as in the poem?" Then he grinned at me.

It was then that I noticed that Juan had both legs amputated. I had not noticed it before because he was floating in the air, with his face at the same height as it would have been if he still had his legs and was standing on the ground.

"Juan, are you here to tell me something?"

"Yes, that you are in danger. The Company is all powerful in Jerome. You know that already, but what you don't know is that they have many ways to kill you. That's what your friend Charlie Vasquez is trying to tell you. He wants to save you from getting killed by them, just as your grandmother and I got killed."

"How did you die Juan?"

"I got my legs burned off trying to save a man who had fallen down in front of a stream of molten copper. They took me to the Company hospital, and a good doctor saved my life, but he couldn't save my legs. I knew that I would never work again. And if you can't work, you are of no use to the Company. They don't want you, and they don't want to take care of you for the rest of your life. For the Company, it's a very simple easy decision. They get rid of you one way or another. With me, they just kicked me out of the hospital and let gangrene do the rest. But I died in such a way that I didn't have to suffer too much. That's all I can tell you about that. But you had better listen to your friend Charlie who is trying to help you." After that, Juan too, was gone.

Bobby addressed the voice behind him, without turning his head. "Are there more than two ghosts here in Jerome?"

"Of course there are more than two. There are more than 200, more than 2000. Jerome has been producing ghosts ever since the mines became big business and that happened very early. At some point it became apparent to the people in control, the ones who were managing the money, that mining was a business in which accidents and deaths occurred quite often. They realized that those deaths and accidents directly affected the margin of profit, and that they could never make as much profit as they wanted to make if they had to take long-term care of injured miners, especially those with no hope of recovery, like Juan de la Cruz. They didn't kill outright, but they just left many to die of neglect. Sometimes they paid a small sum to the family of miners, enough to pay their way out of town. This gave the Company a fixed cost that was included as part of the operating cost of the mining business. A death was followed by a simple bookkeeping entry. Sounds quite cold doesn't it?"

The ghost continued, "Of course, that accounting entry does not take into consideration the feelings, emotion, the frustrations, and the anger of some of the men who died. Those injured men knew that they could have continued to live, had they received better care. But for the mining companies, it was cheaper for them to die.

"It is the energy of the emotions of those who die frustrated, helpless and angry that creates a ghost, and many ghosts have been created around here. That is why there are so many, especially around the hospitals, where many of them spent their last days in your world, alone, helpless, wanting help and not getting it.

"You probably see ghosts without being aware of it, because some ghosts look like real people. You need not be afraid of them, since they can't hurt you. They need a very special dispensation to interact with people, and that privilege is granted to a very special few and on very rare occasions. One more thing. Since time has no meaning on our side, many of these ghosts are still around, even if they died a long time ago, and they will be around a long time to come."

"You must have gotten a special dispensation, or else we would not be here tonight."

"That is true. You are very perceptive. You'll know why I have received a dispensation when I tell you about myself."

"I know what you're trying to teach me, that the Company is very powerful. But I don't think I can take anymore of this tonight. I already know that."

"That is the message that I want to convey, but you still don't know how powerful the mining companies really are, and how their power can be applied against you personally. That's why I am here. Can you come again tomorrow night? Then I will tell you about myself."

The following evening Bobby was in the appointed place. Without looking back, he asked, "Are you there, Charlie?"

"So you found out who I am?"

"Juan told me."

"Does Charlie Vasquez mean anything to you?"

"No, not that I can think of."

"I was five years older than you so I graduated before you reached high school. I died about five years ago, so I'm not surprised that you don't know me. But the story of my life and my death, could well apply to you. That is why I have come to talk to you."

"Charlie, I assure you that you have my full attention."

"Fine, let's get started. You know the story of Romeo and Juliet, don't you?

"Yes."

"Well, if that story had been set in Jerome, it would not have been the Montagues and the Capulets, it would have been a tragedy involving a Vasquez and a Gibson. That's what happened to me. I fell in love with a girl named Betty Gibson and she fell in love with me. Are you in love with Margie?"

"How do you know about her?"

"You've been going together a couple years now, you sit together in the movies, you walk together, you ride bicycles together on Clark Street. And you don't think that a whole bunch of people know about you? Forgive me, I didn't intend to lecture you or criticize you, simply because I made the same mistake. Are you in love with her?"

"To be honest, I think I am, but then I really don't know what love is. I just know that I like the way she smells, the way she talks, the way she looks, the way I feel good when she's around. I even think that I would like to marry her."

"I know what you mean, and you are clearly in love. I felt the same way about Betty. Do her parents know about you?"

"I don't think so. Her mother may have some suspicions, but that is all."

"In these kinds of cases, a suspicion is enough. Positive proof is not necessary. But in my case, her parents did find out and somehow it became known at the Company. My friends had warned me that I was playing with fire, but I stupidly believed no one would find out, that nothing would happen. Boy was I wrong! But let me ask you something. Are you doing it with her? You two have been together plenty of times."

"No, we're not. We have hugged real close, but that is as far as we've gone."

"Maybe that's what has saved you so far. With us, we got caught by her mother in her own house. Her mother told her father who works for the Company. What happened after that, I thought could have been total coincidence. But now I know that they were not coincidences at all, that it was all part of a plan to get rid of me.

"This is what happened. Not long after we were discovered, some strange things occurred. Within a couple of weeks, my father was killed in the mine. The death certificate said it was a mining accident, but that didn't tell me much. We found out later that a rock had fallen on him and had broken his neck, which was somewhat unusual. I should have known then that it was a warning, and that the thing I should have done was to leave town right away. But how could I leave Betty? How could I leave my mother alone to raise my brothers and sisters? And you know that the families of miners have always lived paycheck to paycheck, so we did not have any money to leave town, even if we had decided to do that."

Charlie's voice got quieter. "Next, a man from the Company offered me a job in the mine. I was so stupid that I thought he was trying to help us and was doing us a favor. I took the job, and I was proud that I could take my father's place and provide support for my family.

"My first and only job was that of a mucker. I was given the job of pulling chutes on the 3500-foot level. You know what a chute is, don't you?

"Well, kind of."

"A chute is a hole lined with timbers that is used to drop ore from one level to another farther down, to fill an ore car. The ore cars are formed in a train that hauls the ore out to the surface, and then to the smelter. The chute at the bottom has a wooden door that you open just long enough to let ore out of the chute; then you close the door to the chute when the ore car is full. If you're not careful, the ore keeps coming out faster and faster, making it harder and harder to close the door. The ore can come out fast enough to fill the car, then fill the tunnel, and bury you as well.

"Nobody told me that in a chute with a heavy top cap, that is a chute with heavy ore at the top end, the ore comes out faster than usual, and speeds up very quickly. Nobody told me that I was supposed to attach a safety cable to myself, so that if I got buried, rescuers could find me by following the cable. In brief I was buried by a chute with a heavy top cap.

"When help came, they followed the safety cable to the end, but they did not find me since I had not put it on. They assumed that I had gotten out of the way of the ore and had avoided being buried. But I hadn't been able to do that. I was quickly buried under the ore, and my body was partially under the ore car. Nobody saw me under there. The men who came to look for me cleared away enough ore to convince themselves that I had not been buried by the chute.

"They moved the train, and as the train moved away, it severed my head! They found my body on the tracks, but my head went to the smelter! That is why I did not want you to see me. I have no head! Juan de la Cruz kiddingly calls me 'Headless Charlie.'

"Now, it is possible that all the things that caused my death could have been just coincidences. But it really was part of a plan to get rid of me. The plan worked, because nobody can prove that it was anything but an accident that happened to a careless miner. That type of accident happens frequently, otherwise there would not be a need for the safety cable. The part about cutting off my head was not planned, but the rest of it was."

"I am really sorry that happened to you, Charlie. But that can't happen to me. I don't plan to go anywhere near the mine."

"No, you're not safe. You only think you are. Don't ask me how I know, but they are planning to come after you in an entirely different way. They intend to ship you off to Fort Grant as an incorrigible juvenile. First they will arrest you on some trumped-up charge, the court will find that you are incorrigible, and you will be on your way. The Company owns everyone, the police, the judge, so it is a very simple matter to get you sent away to Fort Grant. Fort Grant is like hell, and no person that is sent there ever comes out the same. You will wish instead that your head had been cut off like my mine."

Bobby was silent and then said, "Charlie, I would hang myself before I would go to Fort Grant. I've heard enough horror stories that scare me even worse than ghosts. Please tell me, what should I do?"

"You need to get out of Jerome as quickly as you can!"

"I could join the Army after graduation."

"Don't waste a single day, and don't let anyone know your plan! Do you see now why I intervened to help you?"

"Of course. I am just lucky that you cared enough to help."

"I helped you for the sake of love. In fact, your Nana and Juan de la Cruz also came for the same reason. We don't like to see innocent love end tragically. That is why we got special dispensation to intervene."

" I can't thank you enough for all that you have shown me. Will I ever see you again?"

"No, if you leave Jerome safely, our job is done."

After that, there was only silence.

GROWING UP IN JEROME

Jerome, Arizona
August, 1945

Sergeant Cruz Rabago
Army Serial Number 93867339
Army Post Office 281
New York, New York

Dear Brother,

  I wish you were here. We sure miss you. Since Papa went to California, and you went away to the Army, that leaves me as the "man of the house." I am really saying that as a joke. Thanks for sending us that money every month. I do not know what we would do without it. Papa is sending some from California, too. But not very much.

  I have been trying to help support the family too, but I am doing a lousy job. I worked for a while at the Western Union Office, and I got 25 cents for each telegram I delivered. I think I earned those 25 cents, because it is a long way from the Western Union Office all the way to the bottom of The Gulch, or to Mexican Town. Those were the parts of Jerome where most of those "We regret to inform you..." telegrams were sent.

But I had to quit, because it was not worth the grief. I would go to deliver a telegram, but the lady of the house would see me before I got to her door. She would come to the door crying. It just got to me and I quit.

After that, I worked one day on the milk delivery truck. Not even one day, really, because I only worked the first stop. I was supposed to jump off the truck while it was still moving, then run to deliver eight quarts of milk, four bottles in each wire basket, to the doorstep of the first houses. My problem was that I did not know that I had to jump off running, in order to land on the ground at the same speed as the truck. Once on the ground, I was supposed to slow down gradually. But I did not do that. I stepped off the truck without running, so wham! The ground went out from under me. I went one way and the broken glass went another way, the milk went flying, and the wire basket also went its separate way. The milkman didn't even let me get back on the truck.

Now I have a job sweeping out Krause's Shoe Store every day. You remember it don't you? A couple of doors away from the Post Office. I get 25 cents a week, which is pretty good. All I do is throw some sawdust with oil on the floor, then sweep it up. I don't give all my money to Mama, though. I keep some of it for myself, to buy a soda, or gum or I spend 11 cents to go to the movie at the Ritz once in a while. I think she knows but she doesn't say anything.

Your loving brother

Jerome, Arizona
September, 1945

Dear Brother,

Gee, I didn't mean to cause you any more worries than you already have. Sure, we're poor, but everyone else in Jerome is poor too. It's not as bad as if we were the only poor family in town. Last week the boss Joe Selna caught Al Cuaron and Cruz Hernandez throwing vegetables out the back window of his store. They were throwing the food down three stories to the street below, the street that goes by the cribs and down to Mexican Town. They had friends down there catching the produce they threw, like heads of lettuce and cabbage. Earlier they had tried throwing tomatoes, but that did not work too well, even if they were able to catch them in the air. Joe was nice enough not to fire them and let them continue to work in the store, after they both promised not to do it anymore. Joe knew they were just trying to get some food for their families.

But the tricks with the produce truck are still going on. You know how Main Street gets real steep at the Union Meat Market, and is steep all the way uphill, past the old elementary school and the Jerome Transfer until you get to the Jerome Hotel? I can't believe that someone has not caught on to what is happening, and put a stop to it. So the truck still comes every Monday morning, that same stake-bed truck that is loaded with produce all the way to the top stake. With the truck so loaded, the driver needs to use low gear to get up the hill. The truck moves so slowly that the boys hide off the road until the truck comes by, then two boys run to catch up to it and climb onto the back bumper. They hold on with one hand, and with the other hand throw produce to other boys running directly behind the truck where the driver can't see them. Once in a while they get lucky and even get a whole sack of potatoes! I can't believe they have not caught onto this scheme, and I hope they don't, because a lot of families are dependent on it.

Some things are changing in town. The big news is that the Jerome Bakery is closing down. I am sure going to miss it. I remember going into the bakery early in the morning to get some fresh potato doughnuts for Papa's lunch. At that time of the morning the whole town was covered in blue smoke from the wood fires in its cooking stoves. What a great feeling it was to go into the bakery when it was cold outside, and feel the warmth and the good smell coming from those big ovens, especially when the bakers had just opened the oven doors to pull out the bread! All that is ending now. No more 5 cent loaves of bread, no more of those great potato doughnuts. The bread now will be coming from Phoenix. I know nobody in Phoenix can duplicate the Jerome Bakery potato doughnuts. I heard that the recipe for them is an old family recipe, and I believe that, because I have never tasted doughnuts that good. Same as the tacos from the Copper Star restaurant. I bet that is an old family recipe also, because you can't get tacos that good anywhere else, can you?

Do you get to eat any local foods, wherever you are, or do you just eat Army chow, as you call it? I could send you some of Mama's tortillas, but by the time you received them they would be more like crackers. Eat your heart out! I still get warm tortillas and beans every day. I like them just plain, not with mayonnaise the way you like them. Mama's tortillas are as good as ever, especially straight off the stove. We still smear a little lard and salt on them while they are still hot. I hope that I am making your mouth water, so that you will not forget the good things here, and will come back soon and safely.

I know that you will not come back to work in the mine. I remember the short time you worked in the mine, before you were drafted. You would come home about 1 am from working the swing shift. You would sleep well for about an hour, and then you would scare the hell out of me screaming things like, "It's coming down! That cable is going to break! Watch out!" You won't remember that, though, because I don't think that you ever fully woke up. You certainly kept me awake, though. Remembering those things makes me wonder: would you choose the Army or the mine, if you were given a choice? I think that I would choose the Army, if I had to choose. Am I being too dumb?

Your loving brother

Jerome, Arizona
September, 1945

Dear Brother,

We have a new teacher this year, Miss Ojeda. She teaches Spanish and she is the first Mexican teacher that I have ever had. Did you ever have any? I'm taking her class and she is pretty good. Pretty and good. She walked into the classroom and started writing on the front blackboard, Parangaricutininimicuaro. She was writing big, so she filled up the front blackboard and continued onto the side blackboard before she had it all spelled out. She said that was the name of a town in Mexico that she had visited over the summer. I was impressed. At least she pronounces "*de*" as we pronounce it, and not "day" as the substitute teacher pronounces it. Most of the students in her class are Mexican and speak Spanish better than they do English, but they still play dumb, even if they know the correct answer, because no one wants to get the reputation of being a *lambion* or as they say in English, an "ass-kisser."

The classes are pretty well mixed, "Americans" and "Mexicans" together, because there are not enough students to have separate classes, as they had in the old days. But still, the white kids are transported on the school bus to the 300- and 500-levels; while the rest of us walk. The American kids still go to the Post Office Cigar Store, while the Mexican kids hang out at Abel's. Same old thing. But listen to this. Phelps Dodge said Mexicans could use the American swimming pool at the 300-level, but only on the day before they changed the water in the pool! Same old thing. No Mexicans have used the pool under those conditions. Anyway, it is more fun swimming in the river at Tapco, or in Oak Creek.

Another thing that has not changed is that here in Jerome a guy still has to prove not only that he is not a lambion, but more importantly that he is not a sissy, not a *joto*.

You cannot hold your head up in this town, with all the miners around, and not be influenced by their toughness. There are still only two ways to prove yourself: either be a good fighter or a good football player. I know that I am not a fighter. I never won one fight against you. The Mexican boys still meet to fight after school in front of the garages on the road to the Little Daisy mine. I'm not sure what I'm going to do, fight or play football.

Your loving brother

Jerome, Arizona
September, 1945

Dear Brother,

I went out for football earlier this month. It sure as hell isn't easy! I'm not sure that I can last, or whether I will make the team. The practice field is the parking lot behind the school gymnasium. I asked the coach why the field was so hard, and he said, "To build character! If you can play on this stuff you can play anywhere!"

The *caliche* is so hard that the shoe cleats barely bite into the ground, and they make almost the same sound as they do on cement. The first week they made us run so much that nearly all of us were throwing up. That reminded me of your letter that you sent me when you were in basic training and said that many soldiers were throwing up on a forced march.

The following week we practiced on our game field which is on the 300-foot level. That field is made from the waste rock of the open pit, with some smaller crushed rock on the surface. Most of the rocks bigger than a golf ball have been screened out, but the smaller ones have a jagged surface, and whenever I break my fall with my hands, I get a scrape that takes the top layer of skin off. The field still has some patches where the cleats don't bite. We Jerome players have learned quickly to avoid those spots, but the visiting players have to learn the hard way.

The coach is still building our characters. I got knocked backwards and hit the back of my head on the hard ground. No sympathy at all from him. All he said was, "Why don't you learn to tuck your chin into your chest before you fall, dummy!" I'm still building my character, I guess.

Your loving brother

Jerome, Arizona
September, 1945

Dear Brother,

Guess what? I made the team! Not that it is a great accomplishment, because there are only forty-four boys in the whole school, and you need at least twenty-two players, so to begin with, I had a fifty-fifty chance. But we don't even have twenty- two good players, so some of us have to play on both defense and offense. There are only five American players over all; I guess they don't have so much to prove. I play on both offense and defense, and have acquired the reputation of being a hard tackler, so I can hold my head up in this town with no problem. After one of the practices, I heard one of the players, a guy named Freddie tell his friend Cuco, "Let's beat up this guy (me) after practice." Cuco told him to forget it. Both of them are tough guys from Mexican Town, and either one of those alone would have been a real challenge, but they thought that they needed both of them to deal with me! Having a tough reputation sure is great!

Even the girls are paying attention to me. Well, one girl. I was at my locker and this girl named Artemisa came and chatted a bit, and then she said to me, "If you will be my boyfriend, I will give you all the (mumble) you want." I didn't hear clearly what she said when she mumbled, so I hesitated. I could tell from her expression that she expected me to say something. But I was still unsure of what she had said, so I decided to play it safe, and told her, "Let me think about it. But how about a free sample of whatever you are offering." She didn't like that, I guess, because she walked off in a huff and hasn't spoken to me since.

I told you in my last letter that we would be playing our first game against Kingman, here in Jerome, on our home field. The Kingman team plays on grass at home. Kingman's football uniforms looked perfect, except for a grass stain here and there. Not like our uniforms. Ours are all torn and ragged from the hard, rocky field. Our game uniforms don't look too bad from a distance, but up close they don't look very good. I think that adds to our tough reputation.

While we were getting suited up in our game uniforms, one of our players, a guy named Beanses came in late. He came through the door yelling, "We are going to beat the *chit* out of them! We are going to beat the chit out of them!"

He told us that the Kingman players were already suited up, that they were already on our playing field, and that they were trying to clear all the rocks off the field!

He said, "I'm not kidding you! Their coach has them spaced out on one of the side lines. Then they all walk parallel to each other, all the way across the field to the other sideline, each player trying to pick up every rock in his path! They can never get all the rocks off the field! Each player gets an armful of rocks, more than he can carry, before he is even halfway across! So each player is getting a close look at the field that they are going to be falling on, and they are going to chit their pants before the game even starts! We're going to beat the chit out of them!"

Even our coach decided that he could not give us a better motivational speech than that, so he simply said, "Let's go whip them!" We got onto the bus with total confidence, and during the game we played as if we were invincible. Of course we won.

Your invincible loving brother

Joe Stamsek

JEROME, ARIZONA, December 7, 1941:

I saw my friend Arturo walking with long strides, as if he were late for Mass. I could see him from where I was sitting on the front porch of my house on Clark Street. It was a sunny day, very warm for December. The town was quiet, as it usually was on Sunday mornings.

Arturo came around the corner on School Street, from the direction of the Jerome Bakery. It was close to eleven o'clock in the morning, so I knew that no matter how fast Arturo walked, he would not make it to the church in time for the last Mass of the day, which had started at ten o'clock. I could hear his rapid breathing as he turned onto the short path that led uphill to my house. Just by looking at him, I knew that he must have something important to tell me. And he did.

Almost out of breath, and well before he reached me, he called out, "Pache, have you heard? The Japanese have bombed Pearl Harbor!"

I didn't know how to react. I was only fifteen years

old at the time, and I did not know the implication of his words. For one thing, Pearl Harbor did not mean anything to me. I did not even know where it was located. The most distant place that I knew was Phoenix. If Pearl Harbor was farther away than Phoenix, I was not too concerned.

Arturo gave me some details. He said that bombs from Japanese planes had killed a lot of soldiers and sailors, and had sunk a bunch of ships. But not until he told me that the USS Arizona was one of the ships that was hit, and that it was still burning, did the seriousness of Arturo's news begin to sink in.

"How do you know all this, Arturo?"

"I heard it from a Phoenix radio station. You must not have had your radio turned on."

"You're right. I'll go turn it on now!"

As I turned to go inside, I saw my mother standing in the doorway with a shocked look on her face. She could not understand English, so she could not have understood everything Arturo had said. But she had picked up enough meaning to know that the news was bad. I explained to her in Spanish what Arturo had said. Her first question to me was, "How long will this war last?" Probably every mother in Jerome who had young sons was asking that same question as they heard the news.

I asked her permission to go tell my friend Joe Stamsek the news. Even though I was fifteen years old, it was still my custom to ask my mother's permission to leave the house. Although Arturo had addressed me as "Pache," that was only my nickname. Everybody called me that; everyone except my teachers. Even some of my friends did not know that my real name was Cruz.

I got my nickname from my older sister Belia. When we were little kids, we were having an ordinary brother-sister fight. She of course was fighting like a girl, and was pulling my hair, hard. To defend myself, I shoved her away, maybe harder than I should have, but she was really hurting me. As she was falling backwards, she yelled at me, "You're an Apache!" She meant it as an insult, but I took it as a compliment, and that must have showed on my face, so she kept calling me that, and the name has stuck with me ever since.

I took my sister's insult as a compliment because the Apache warriors were some of the fiercest fighters the world has ever known. I guess every boy would like to cause fear in his enemies just by his appearance and reputation. Little did my sister know that in my imagination I would become Chief Geronimo, charging on a white horse into battle, riding bareback, directing my horse with my knees and my fellow warriors with a wave of one hand, while firing a rifle with the other, weaving through bullets and arrows that were aimed at me, but that always missed. But these things were in my imagination, because in real life I was not mean nor fierce, and I knew that the bullets and arrows don't always miss.

There was no fence between Joe Stamsek's house and mine, so Arturo and I crossed from my yard into Joe Stamsek's yard. Joe was not only my neighbor, he was my best friend, my companion, my role model. He was a year older than I, but he seemed to know everything. I thought that he was smarter in many ways than my teachers, and I probably learned more things from Joe than I learned in school. Joe knew practical things, like why a mammal shivers when it is cold, and why a cup of coffee cools faster if you leave the spoon in the coffee.

But his real passion was the airplane, the model airplane kind. He could design them, build them and fly them. He knew all about the aerodynamics of the airflow over the wing shape that produced the lift. He could calculate the amount of wing surface area to support a model engine of a given weight, the area of a control surface necessary at different speeds, and all kinds of things like that. We got along well because we were neighbors, close to the same age, and he knew that I, too, liked to take things apart to see how they worked, then put them back together.

Arturo and I found Joe in his workshop, where you could always find him. It was a small room that Joe had made, with two large windows for light, and one bare bulb for light when there was no sun. The room had no running water, no heating or cooling, but Joe worked there all year round. The room contained one large work table, one chair, and about ten model airplanes all over the room, some suspended from the ceiling. The room smelled of airplane glue and exhaust smoke from one of the small motors that Joe had been testing earlier.

Joe was bent over the work table, with an Exacto knife between his thumb and first finger, making a delicate cut into some balsa wood that he was shaping to match the blueprint tacked to the table.

Joe looked like a surgeon, and it was easy to imagine that the Exacto knife was a scalpel, and that he was performing an operation. His hands were that delicate, and they matched his slim face and body. Muscles were probably the one thing that I had more of, compared to Joe. When we walked into his room, Joe looked up briefly and said, "Give me a moment to finish this cut."

When we told Joe the news, he said, "Do you mean the Japanese are extending their zone of aggression? Do they know what they are doing taking on this country?" But of course, neither of us knew. After some more discussion, I told Joe that my mother wanted me to be certain that his mother knew the news. Joe said, "Let's all go upstairs to tell her."

Joe's mother was named Feliciana, but it seems like most people in Jerome had a nickname, and hers was "Chana." Feliciana means "happy woman," but she did not look happy after we told her the news.

She said, "I don't like this at all, boys. I know that you have told me that Pearl Harbor is far away from Jerome, but when a war starts, nobody can control it, and who knows where it may spread. Don't think that it could not reach Jerome! I can see that you are all excited about this, but I don't want you to get carried away, because you do not have any idea what war can be like. I will tell you that it is not just uniforms and parades, it is ugly and brutal."

She must have been reading my mind, because I had been thinking, "I wonder what an old lady knows about war?"

She looked directly at me when she said, "All wars are the same. They all involve fighting and crying and bleeding and dying. Yes, I have seen war. I was a young girl in Mexico during the time of the Revolution there. I don't want to think about it, but I will tell you this much. There was fighting all around the little town where I lived. I took food, and the boys my age took water to the men who were fighting in the trenches. But bullets don't care if you are a boy or a girl or a man. I saw men, women and children blown apart, some bleeding to death without anyone to console them or bless them. It is a lonely, horrible way to die. I just hope that this war does not last long enough for it to reach any of you, and that you all get to die of old age."

She could not hold back her sorrow, and started crying without restraint. Arturo and I left. Joe stayed behind and put his arm around his mother, not saying a word.

Joe was different than most of his friends in Jerome; even his name was different—Stamsek. His friends were surnamed Quintero, Garcia, Gonzalez, Hernandez and other typical "Mexican" names. None of them were really Mexican, for they had all been born in Jerome and of course all of them were American citizens. But that did not matter much in Jerome. If your parents, grandparents, or even five or more generations back were born in Mexico, then you were Mexican. That put you in a different category or class, not as good, as the "Americans."

Joe's father was the handyman for the chief surgeon's house, but Joe's mother and father were no longer married to each other. His mother's present husband was surnamed Enriquez and Joe had two half-brothers and a sister with that surname. As a result, Joe had a foot in each of the two ethnic groups in Jerome, and he was well liked by both groups.

After Pearl Harbor, the excitement of war stayed high in Jerome, and we followed its progress by reading the headlines of *The Arizona Republic* in the newsstand, without buying the paper. On other occasions, we went to the Ritz Theater, the only theater in Jerome, to see the "Movietone News," which were newsreels about the war. They were of great interest, even if they were weeks behind the current events. Even so, they conveyed the news that the battles in the Pacific Islands were moving closer to the Japanese mainland; that the battles in North Africa were over, and that the active combat zones had moved from Sicily into the mainland of Italy. We knew that it was only a matter of time until the battle for France would begin, but we did not know how or when.

We felt, as did everybody, that Jerome was an important part of the War Effort, because the output of the mine was so important. We knew that copper was used to make bullets and shells, and was vital to communications equipment. Proof of Jerome's importance was that men with weapons guarded the entrance to the mine, and miners had to present identification cards with their picture before they could enter. Jerome houses were required to have blackout curtains to make it more difficult for German bombers to locate the mine, should they decide to cripple the War Effort by bombing it. However, no German bombers ever reached Jerome. Still the feeling that we were helping to win the war made it easier to endure food and gasoline rationing, to give up meat and butter, and to drink coffee made over and over from the same grounds.

Joe and I continued our lives much in the same way as before the war started. We both stayed in school. Joe continued to build his model airplanes. I became interested in crystal radios and photography. I even developed my own photographs.

One day Joe and I went to the football field on the 300-foot level to flight test one of the larger models that Joe had built. Joe said that this was not to be a full-fledged test flight, but only a preliminary flight to adjust what he called the vertical and horizontal stabilizer trim settings, and the dihedral. He patiently explained to me that he wanted to set the trim so that the model in free flight would fly in a circle, rather than having it fly off in a straight line until it ran out of gas and we might not be able to find it.

The horizontal stabilizer trim, he said, was to achieve a slight nose-up attitude when the plane was in flight, to balance the weight of the engine in the front. The hardest thing for me to understand was dihedral, which he said was the angle that the wings made with the horizontal. The preliminary test flight was successful. The next flight would be the full-fledged test flight, but we would have to postpone that for another day.

As we were getting ready to start back home, Joe seemed lost in thought for a few moments. Then he said to me, "Pache, what do you think of the idea of putting one of your crystal radios in this model? If we could figure out a way to send radio commands to the receiver in the plane, we could control the flight from the ground, and make it do all kinds of maneuvers. What do you think?"

I said, "I think that is a great idea, but it would be really complicated to carry out. I suggest that we give your idea a name, so that we can think about it as we go along. How about EX-1?"

Joe said, "EX for experimental? Since we're doing it together, I think that we should name it the EX-2!"

I knew then that Joe and I were really partners, not just best friends.

As we were walking back home, Joe asked me how often I changed my socks. I told him once a week. He said that he hoped my week was up for those socks. At first, I was offended, but I quickly realized that only a true friend would tell me that my feet smelled. But I did change my socks when I got home.

Meanwhile, World War II continued. The battles were becoming fiercer, and ever harder to win. The war in the Pacific was in fact moving closer to Japan, but each island came at a higher price in the number of lives lost. The war in Italy stagnated; more and more soldiers died, but not much territory was gained.

The war was coming ever closer to Jerome. Joe Stamsek was nearing his eighteenth birthday. Three years before, President Roosevelt had signed into law the Selective Service Act of 1940, commonly known as the draft. The Act was the means of supplying the ever-increasing needs of the military for young men to fight the war. Every male was required to register for the draft upon reaching his eighteenth birthday.

The number of men who were drafted varied according to the needs of the military services. At the beginning of the war, only a small number of men were drafted, because the military did not have a place to train them. But after the training facilities were built, and the combat intensified, more and more men were called up, not only for present military needs, but also for anticipated requirements.

Local draft boards were established to administer the draft, one draft board for each county across the nation, staffed locally with leading citizens. The draft board for Jerome was located in Prescott, on the other side of Mingus Mountain. The local boards had wide discretion to determine who would be called, who would be deferred or exempted, and who would be drafted.

Joe Stamsek registered when he turned eighteen years old. That brought Joe into the vast machinery of the military conscription for World War II. From then on, he was subject to forces that were beyond his control.

A MEETING OF THE SELECTIVE
SERVICE BOARD OF YAVAPAI COUNTY,
PRESCOTT ARIZONA, SPRING OF 1943.

TEMPORARY CHAIRMAN: Good evening. I am just filling in for the chairman. We have a lot of work to do tonight, so I will try to move us right along. Our first order of business is to develop a list of thirty names for the next batch of draftees. This agenda item is now open for preliminary discussion.

NEW MEMBER: Mr. Chairman, I propose that all eligible names be put in a hat, and then drawn out, sight unseen, so that way thirty names would be chosen at random.

OLD MEMBER 1: Afraid not, son. We would not be doing our job then. Everything would be left to chance, and heaven forbid, it would be possible that all thirty names would all be from our own home town of Prescott. Now we would not want that to happen, would we? We can't have that. Better we keep control of the process.

CHAIRMAN: I agree. Since I am only a temporary chairman, this is not the time to be making any big changes. I don't think we even have to take a vote on that. We will just keep using the same procedure. So let us get on with this business. We need to come up with thirty names to make up the next batch of draftees.

OLD MEMBER 2: Question, Mr. Chairman. So we will continue to use the same formula?

CHAIRMAN: Well yes. But I don't want to leave an impression on the record that we have a formula, because we don't. But when a name comes up, each of us can give his input, or an opinion, especially if we know the young man, or his family. After that we vote to accept the name, reject it, or defer it, according to our conscience. But we must keep in mind our responsibilities. Don't forget that we might be sending these boys to their deaths. It is a hell of a responsibility, but we are all here to do our job as good citizens. Let's get on with it. Mr. Secretary, would you please read the next name on the list, starting from where we left off at the last meeting?

SECRETARY: Number 746, James Robinson, age nineteen, Prescott.

CHAIRMAN: Anybody know him?

OLD MEMBER 3: Yes, he's from my neck of the woods. He is a good friend of my son I think that he is a likely candidate for a deferment, so he would not ultimately fulfill our quota. Can we go onto the next name?

CHAIRMAN: Next name, please.
SECRETARY: Number 1644, Jesus Rodriguez, age eighteen, Jerome.

CHAIRMAN: Does anybody know this young man from Jerome? Hearing no response, the Chair is open to a vote or further comments.

OLD MEMBER 1: I move we add Jesus Rodriguez to the list.

OLD MEMBER 4: I second the motion.

CHAIRMAN: I, of course, am willing to do whatever you members want to do, but I would like to point out that we have already added too many Gonzalez's and Lopez's and that kind of name from Jerome, and we cannot give the impression that we are being anything but totally fair.

OLD MEMBER 4: I withdraw my second. May the secretary read the next name on the list?
SECRETARY: Number 550, Joe Stamsek, age eighteen, from Jerome.

OLD MEMBER 5: What kind of a name is that?

OLD MEMBER 7: Sounds Czech to me.

OLD MEMBER 8: Czech. Aren't they on the German side now?

After a brief discussion, Joe Stamsek's name was included in the next list of men to be drafted.

Thus it came to pass that Joe Stamsek, along with eight of his classmates, (there were only seventeen men in the class), received an order to report for induction into the Armed Forces of the United States of America. They were all considered Mexican. They were ordered to report to the Induction Station in Phoenix, Arizona, on May 30, 1943, two days after their high school graduation. They were advised to bring sufficient clothing for three days. For the Jerome men, this meant one pair of Levi's, one shirt, one pair of shoes, and one set of underwear. In other words, the clothes they were wearing, because they only owned one set of clothes at any time.

On May 29th, Joe Stamsek's sister and I were part of the small crowd that gathered on Main Street to wish farewell to the group of Jerome soldiers. There were a lot of tears and heavy hearts, but everyone tried to put on a brave face. The Santa Fe Trailways morning bus arrived, and the men boarded one by one. Joe Stamsek was the last to board, after he had told me that he would write to me if he could.

He wrote his first postcard to me while he was still at the Induction Station. He said that the first few days were pleasant, because all the Jerome men stayed with each other, and that made it seem that they were still at home. But he was also glad and sad that he was going to separate from them. He was glad, because he had scored very well on the Army IQ test, had been selected to attend Officer's Candidate School in the Army Air Corps, and would get to be around real airplanes! But he said that he was sad because the other Jerome soldiers were going into infantry training, and he was afraid that he might never see them again.

For me, Jerome was not the same with Joe gone. My friend Arturo had also left town, but he had moved to California with his family. His family had moved to the Los Angeles area to work in one of the defense plants. I must have continued to do much the same things as before, because I don't recall anything significant in that year before I turned eighteen myself, on May 3, 1944. I remember that well, because one month later, it was my turn to be on the Santa Fe bus to the Phoenix Induction Station.

Two weeks later, I was assigned to infantry training at Camp Roberts, California. Infantry training was seventeen weeks of the most intense physical and military training. I gained thirty pounds of muscle. I was put through forced marches of eighteen miles carrying a rifle and a sixty-pound field pack. I received bayonet training and marksmanship training. I had been prepared as a combat soldier. When I finished the five months of infantry training, I was given a two-week furlough at home, before going to my next assignment. I was most anxious to go home.

Two days before I left for home on my two-week leave, I received a letter from Joe that did not make any sense to me. The letter had been heavily censored by the military censor, with patches of black ink to obliterate the words that the censor found impermissible. There was no way to date the letter, because even the date had been blanked out. From the condition of the letter, it was probable that it had been delayed for some months. I kept the letter anyway, simply because it was a letter from Joe. I carried it in my pocket.

The letter said: "Things are really (blank) for me. (blank). (blank) more (blank)(blank) (blank) amount of (blank) (blank). We are (blank) our way (blank)(blank). Wish me luck. Your best friend, Joe."

I finished my training, and headed for Jerome on

my first leave. I had expected to arrive in Jerome on the morning bus, but I had missed a connection in Los Angeles, so I did not arrive in Jerome until the evening bus, and there was no one there to meet me. I didn't speak to anyone as I headed straight for home.

My way home took me past Joe Stamsek's house, and I noticed that his house was dark, empty and silent. As soon as I reached home, my family engulfed me.

"You don't know how glad we are to see you! We thought you weren't coming, when you weren't on the morning bus! You look so strong! My little boy has become a man! Welcome home!"

As soon as these words of welcome had subsided, I asked my mother, "Where is the Stamsek family?" Immediately my mother turned from joy into sorrow, and she started to cry.   Through her sobs, she said, "You did not know that Joe was killed in France last month? When his mother got the news, she said that she could not stand to live here any more, knowing that her son would never return. They moved to Los Angeles two days later. It has been terribly sad around here. When will this war end? So many families in Jerome have suffered so much!"

She wiped her tears away with her apron and took a deep breath, sighing so deeply I thought the house might rock. Then she said, "Joe's mother left something for you. She told me that in the last letter that she had received from Joe, he had told her to give something to you. I'll go get it." Before I could stop her, she went into the back room off the kitchen and came back holding a large model airplane. On both sides of the fuselage, and on the top of each wing, Joe had painted in precise large black letters in black ink–EX-2.

When I saw that, my throat started to swell. I did not want to cry in front of my mother. I could not say anything without bursting into tears, so I silently took the airplane and headed out the back door towards Joe's old house. When I reached his old workshop, I sat on the bottom step of the entrance and placed the airplane beside me. I took out the strange letter from Joe, and knowing now that he had been killed in France, and with my knowledge of the general progress of the war, I could decipher the strange letter almost as if there had been no words blanked out. I could now read what Joe had tried to say to me:

"Things are really changing for me. No more Officer Candidate Training. My entire class has been re-assigned to an infantry division in (?) We have received a small amount of basic training and are on our way to Europe. Wish me luck. Your best friend, Joe."

I felt a horrible anger rise up in me when I realized what had happened. The "Needs of the Military" had taken some of the brightest young minds out of the Air Corps Officer Training, and because they needed more riflemen in the battle for Europe, they had put them in an infantry division without giving them the necessary physical strengthening or adequate military training in the nitty-gritty dirty details of armed combat. They were shipped off to Europe, where they fought against hardened veteran German soldiers. Against such horrible odds, I was surprised that Joe had survived as long as he had. But that did not make me feel one bit better.

I picked up a rock with my hand and smashed the airplane into a mess of tiny pieces of wood and paper. I threw the letter into the pile, and set fire to it all. I watched everything burn until the smoke had all blown away, the last spark had died out, and nothing remained.

Looking back, I wish that I had not done that.

Postscript

The story of Joe Stamsek is a tragic one. It is made more tragic by the fact that except for a couple of incidents in this story that have been fictionalized, the Joe Stamsek story is true. Joe was a very bright young man; he was very interested in airplanes, he was drafted the day after his graduation; he was accepted into Officer's Candidate School; he was re-assigned to an infantry unit; he died in combat in France within a year and a half of his graduation. His remains are interred in the American Cemetery at Epinal-Vosges.

But there is another larger tragedy. Consider that there were eighteen soldiers from Jerome killed in World War II, and seventy-one soldiers killed from all of Yavapai County. The 1940 census showed only 2,295 people living in Jerome, and a total of 25,511 people living in Yavapai County. This means that 25 per cent of the soldiers that died were from Jerome, yet Jerome only had 8 per cent of the population of Yavapai County!

Why should this have been? Pondering an answer to this question gave rise to the writing of this story.

HERE DEAD LIE WE BECAUSE
WE DID NOT CHOOSE

Here dead lie we because we did not choose,
To live and shame the land from which we sprung.
Life, to be sure, is nothing much to lose;
But young men think it is, and we were young.
A.E. Housman

"Here Dead Lie We Because We Did Not Choose" from the COLLECTED POEMS OF A.E. HOUSMAN. Copyright 1924, 1965 by Henry Holt and Company. Reprinted by permission of Henry Holt and Company, LLC.

Memorial plaque, Jerome, Arizona. Photo by Jamie Moffett.

JEROME SOLDIERS WHO WERE KILLED IN WWII:

Guadalupe D. Chavez
Jesus R. Cuaron, Sam L.
Cvijanovich, Robert Davenport
Adolfo Fritz
Conrado A. Granillo
Frank Giusti
Charles D. Ivey
Antonio M. Madrid
Pilar Muñiz
Thomas C. Muñoz, Gabriel
Olvera, Antonio Perez
Teodosio M. Rodriguez
Robert H. Sanchez
Herbert Schumacher
Joe C. Stamsek
Albert M. Zardaneta

Special thanks to Salvador Muñoz, a World War II veteran from Jerome, now deceased, who was an early and strong advocate for proper recognition of the sacrifices made by Jerome soldiers.

Veteran's Day

The World War II veterans were returning home to Jerome from the European Theater of combat operations. Some had already been in the military service long enough to be discharged back into civilian life; others were coming home for a brief furlough before being re-assigned to the fierce combat of the Pacific islands. Still others were not coming home, ever.

On this day in June, 1945, six veterans of the war in Europe came home to Jerome. This occurred strictly by chance, for they had all been serving in different units, most of them in the infantry, but some had served in the airborne parachute units. They recognized each other as being from the same home town; nevertheless they were quite surprised to encounter each other at the Santa Fe Trailways Bus Depot in Phoenix, and to realize that they were all boarding the same bus back home to Jerome.

The bus arrived in Jerome at seven o'clock in the evening and stopped on Main Street, at the wide spot in the road, at the stone steps below the little park in the center of town, across the street from Paul and Jerry's Saloon. The bus driver unloaded their canvas duffel bags that had their last names and serial numbers painted on the side of each bag. Each soldier picked up his own bag and headed for home, accompanied by their families who were there to greet them.

The next day, though, the families had to share their heroes with the entire town, so the soldiers left their families and went uptown to Main Street, where they could see and be seen. Their presence gave all of Jerome a festive air, as if the Fourth of July, the 16th of September, St. Patrick's Day and New Year's Eve had combined into one holiday. The mood of Jerome on this day was that of Jerome on a payday. Mother Nature had cooperated by producing a glorious sunny day. Germany had done its part by announcing its surrender on May 9th.

The sidewalks were crowded by Jerome standards, and the excited voices of the people could be heard everywhere. There was also the joy of anticipation, because the townspeople sensed that there could be better times ahead, that the time of worry and sadness would end, that Japan would also surrender soon, and the hardships of World War II would finally be over. The presence of the returning soldiers was living proof that Jerome had done its share in contributing to the war effort.

The overall feeling in town was one of joy, but beneath the joy there were many different feelings. Young men close to the age of being drafted felt some relief in the thought that perhaps the war would be over before they would be called. Boys younger than draft age felt a disappointment that they might not be called to serve, might never have the opportunity to come home to receive the adulation and congratulations of their families and friends. Women felt relieved that their sons still at home would be safe. Those mothers with sons who were still serving in the military could hope that their sons, too, would come home safely. In the meantime, they took pride that they too were serving in their own way, and proudly displayed a small flag with a blue star, which indicated that they had a son in the military. The only sad people on this day were women whose windows displayed a gold star in the center of the flag, which meant that the serviceman in the family had been killed in action, and would never be coming home. There were quite a few gold star flags in Jerome, perhaps too many for so small a town.

For a few hours that morning, it seemed as if the usual social structure of the town had been upended by the returning soldiers. The soldiers were all of Hispanic origin, but in those days, they were known as "Mexicans," even though they would not have been drafted had they not been American citizens. But long-standing barriers of ethnicity and social standing were forgotten on this day, and all the soldiers were welcomed as real heroes.

One of the returning soldiers was Mike Lopez, who, before he was drafted, had worked for the Union Meat Market on lower Main Street. His former job had been to drive a small, red Ford pickup to deliver orders of groceries directly to the homes of customers. On this happy morning in June, Mike was walking on Main Street in Jerome, towards the Post Office. He was dressed in his full dress Army uniform, which displayed on his upper left chest the Combat Infantry Man's badge, and below that, a row of ribbons to show that he had fought in most of the campaigns across Europe. Below one of the ribbons hung a Silver Star. Those men who knew that the Silver Star was only awarded to men who had shown "exceptional bravery in combat" made a special effort to shake Mike's hand. Some men would prolong their handshake, all the while looking into his eyes, as if trying to feel what Mike had gone through in combat, trying to see Mike's sorrows, hurts, bravery, and his will to survive. Some men asked him, "What was it like, Mike?" Mike only replied in his controlled, respectful delivery-boy voice, "It is good to be home."

During the morning, one of the arriving soldiers named Reyes Borjon had thoroughly enjoyed being on the receiving end of the good wishes and welcomes that Jerome had given him. He had also drunk more than one of the free beers that had been offered him. Reyes could sense, however, that the brotherly love mood of Jerome was ending with the morning, so he decided to move from the uptown bars to the Copper Star, a Mexican bar and restaurant located on Main Street, farther downhill. Any Mexican born in Jerome could read the crowd and sense when they were not welcome. The mood of brotherhood had shifted and Reyes shifted with it.

As he started down hill, he met up with Mike Lopez, who was walking in the same direction. They exchanged greetings and gave each other an *abrazo*.

Mike asked, "Are you leaving the celebration so soon?"

Reyes responded, "I'm not sure the 'welcome home war heroes' is going to last. I decided to leave before my welcome wore out."

Mike said, "I was feeling the same thing. That's why I'm heading home. I live down in The Gulch. Are you walking that way?"

"I'm just going as far as the Copper Star."

As they got to the door of the bar, Reyes asked Mike, "Why don't you let me buy you a beer?"

Mike answered, "Thanks, Reyes. I think I'll go on

home. You go ahead and have a good time, but take care of yourself."

Reyes grinned and slapped him on the back. "Mike, if I've learned anything in this war, it's to take care of myself." He entered the bar feeling good, as Mike walked on.

Reyes was of normal height, but not of normal build, for he was too broad across the shoulders, too deep in the chest, and too narrow in the waist. His muscles were hardened from the rigors of months of combat in France, Belgium and Germany. He had dressed in his full uniform for his homecoming. His cap displayed a patch with a parachute, and on his left shoulder patch was the Screaming Eagle of the 101st Airborne Division.

Mentally, Reyes was glad to be in a place where he was not in constant danger, where he could be free from having to be on full alert. Reyes felt at ease in the Copper Star. He accepted numerous pats on the back, many arms around his shoulders, and also many glasses of beer. They were stacked on the bar before him, four or five deep, depending on how fast he had finished the last one. Reyes lost his fears, and for the first time in many, many months he felt safe and among friends.

After some time, he knew that he had reached his limit, so he decided to head for home. The men at the bar were reluctant to let him go, until he promised them that he would return later that evening. He went out the door, then headed towards the center of town. He intended to walk past the Post Office, to the stairway that led downhill to Mexican Town, where he lived.

The outside fresh air increased the effect of the alcohol on Reyes and by the time he reached Robinson's Jewelry Store, he was not able to recognize anyone, and he was not totally certain whether he was walking on

Main Street in Jerome, or on the Champs Elysées in Paris. Reyes concluded that he was in his home town, so he followed his instincts to get himself home. He continued on his way, making slow, unsteady progress. He did not always move in a straight line, but he kept moving in the right direction.

The alcohol intensified his emotions. He felt so glad to be alive and well, and back in his own home town. But he also felt some guilt when he thought of his fellow soldiers that would never make it home. Why had he survived while others had not? He had just learned in the bar that his life-long friend and neighbor in Jerome, Jess Cuaron, had been killed in France only two months ago. That made him feel guilty and sad.

Reyes continued walking with his mind in a fog of emotions. At times he could almost perceive his present reality, but at other times he was in a distorted world of alcoholic exaggerations and sentimentalities; sometimes back in his home town, sometimes not. When he reached the center of town, he staggered diagonally across the intersection. He reached the other side and started to turn towards home, but he stopped in front of Shen's Photo Studio, alarmed by the strange chemical odor that wafted from it.

Mr. Shen was an older man of Chinese descent, who had been Jerome's photographer for a long time. He took baptismal photos of infants, then years later photographed the same children as brides in their wedding gowns. He photographed all important festivities of the town, Fourth of July celebrations as well as the 16th of September holidays. Mr. Shen was a quiet man who always dressed in plain-front khaki pants and short-sleeved khaki shirts. His black hair was trimmed square across the bottom. The deep color of his black hair contrasted with the color of his khaki clothing and that gave the skin of his face a yellowish tinge. Problems with his liver also contributed to his yellowish complexion. He wore old-fashioned round glasses that had a thin gold frame. Had his teeth been a little more protruding, and his skin a little more yellow, he would have looked exactly like the demonized caricature of a "Jap" in all the anti-Japanese propaganda films and posters that were intended to stir up hatred of the enemy. Mr. Shen's appearance was normally not a problem, because everyone in Jerome knew him, and knew that he was not the enemy. Unfortunately, on this day, Mr. Shen's appearance did cause a problem for Reyes.

Mr. Shen happened to be standing exactly in the middle of the entrance to his studio, but a few steps back from the sidewalk. His reflection was multiplied by the windows around him. Drunk and confused, Reyes saw Mr. Shen and mistook him for a Japanese enemy. Then, Reyes saw other Japs standing behind and to the side of the Jap in front of him

Reyes reached for the nearest Jap, picked him up and threw him through the window of the studio. Mr. Shen landed on a countertop inside. His face was quickly covered in blood from the cuts on his scalp and forehead. Reyes crouched in a defensive posture outside, still confused, wondering why the other two Japs had not yet attacked and how they had vanished.

Tom, the bad half of Jerome's police force, happened to be two stores away, in front of the Post Office Cigar Store. When he heard the shouting and the breaking of glass, he ran immediately to Shen's Studio. Without stopping to ask any questions, he drew out his two-foot long night stick, raised it above his head and brought it down hard on the top of Reyes' head. Reyes' cap was knocked off his head, but he did not go down. Tom hit him again on his bare head, and this time Reyes went down, bleeding. Unconscious, Reyes slumped sideways.

Blood gushed down his neck onto his shirt, staining the eagle's screaming mouth with streaks of red and turning all of his campaign ribbons crimson.

Tom turned the unconscious Reyes onto his back. He handcuffed his wrists together. Without saying a word, he grabbed hold of the chain that connected the two wrists and dragged Reyes across the sidewalk onto the street. Reyes' head struck the pavement, but Reyes did not react.

Tom dragged Reyes across the street, bumped Reyes' head on the sidewalk on the other side, then drug him to the jail a block away, leaving a trail of blood. When they arrived at the jail, Tom lifted the still unconscious Reyes onto a bare metal slab in the holding cell, and left him there.

And that was the way this Veteran's Day ended.

The Millionaire and the Tamale Lady

As Aurelia leaned over to place another faggot in the fire, out of the corner of her eye she saw a man dressed in black looking intently at her. He was standing alongside a shiny, black four-door sedan with yellow spoke wheels. He must have driven from the highway down the old cemetery road that ran next to her house. She did not know how long the man had been looking at her, because she had been so intent on washing her clothes.

Not many cars came down that road anymore. The cemetery was filled with the victims of the Spanish influenza that had struck Jerome in 1918. No fresh graves had been opened for thirty years. There were few visitors anymore.

As was her custom, she was doing her wash on a Saturday morning, in a round, galvanized tin tub. She had set the tub on rocks high enough to allow a wood fire to burn underneath. The tub was filled with water that she had brought in buckets from her kitchen in the two-room wooden shack where she lived with her husband.

She washed the clothes by first soaking them in the hot soapy water, then scrubbing them by hand against metal riffles in the wooden washboard. She dipped her hand into the water to test whether it was hot enough to get her husband's shirts clean. Aurelia flicked the hot water off fingers hardened by hundreds of tubs of hot soapy water and the daily chores of chopping wood, cleaning and cooking. In spite of Aurelia's hard life and hands toughened by work, she was still a slim, attractive woman.

When she was satisfied that the water was hot enough for washing her husband's shirts, she was ready to start the next phase of her wash.

Aurelia had forgotten about the strange man because she was concentrating on washing her husband's shirts. She took a blue denim shirt out of the water and placed it on the washboard. With both hands, she held the collar of the shirt and scrubbed it up and down against the corrugations. Then she did the same to the front of the shirt, taking care not to hurt the buttons. Finally, she scrubbed the back panel of the shirt, the easy part. When she was satisfied that the shirt was clean, she dropped it into a separate rinse bucket.

She was beginning to wash the next shirt, when she was startled by a man's voice that asked in Spanish, "Is your husband here?"

Aurelia looked up to see that the man in black had approached close enough to address her. He was a well-built man who looked to be in his late 50s, slightly taller than her husband. He had taken off his black hat and held it in front of his waist, with both hands.

Because of his respectful attitude, Aurelia relaxed. She thought to herself, "A well-dressed man like that, with hair already turning gray, would not be seeking to harm a woman like me, with bony arms, wearing an old dress, sweating over a hot tub."

If Aurelia had been afraid, she would have responded that her husband was inside the house. Instead, she told him in Spanish, "He's not here. He walked uptown to get a haircut."

The man replied courteously, "*Muchas gracias*," and walked away, back to his car. From his car, he watched her a while longer, then he drove up the dirt road back to the highway.

Her husband came home as she was hanging his shirts on the outdoor clothesline, securing them to the rope with wooden clothespins. As he approached her, Aurelia looked over her shoulder and said to him, "A man was here looking for you, only a short while ago."

"Oh, really? What did he look like?"

"He was dressed in a black suit, wearing a black hat. He looked like an undertaker."

"Did he come in a car? What kind of car was it?"

"I don't know the kind of car, but it was a new car."

"Was it black?"

"Yes."

"Did he speak Spanish?"

"Yes, he asked me if you were here, in Spanish. He spoke it so well that I did not give it a second thought."

"Did he tell you his name? Did he say why he wanted to see me?"

"No, he didn't say anything else."

"How long ago was he here?"

"About fifteen minutes ago."

"Well, I had better go find him. You don't keep a man like that waiting."

"Who was he?"

"*Ay, señora.* Don't you know? That was Jimmy Douglas!"

"*Ay! Dios mio!*" she said, putting a hand on her forehead. "The millionaire! The owner of the Little Daisy Mine, the owner of our house and the land we live on! Why I didn't even offer him a chair or a cup of coffee! How could I have been so ill-mannered?!"

"Relax, woman. Maybe with some other millionaire there might have been a problem. But not with Jimmy Douglas. He is very human, you know, *muy gente.* He ran the mine in Nacozari, Mexico. He was a good friend of Jesus García."

"Who is Jesus García?"

"Old woman, don't you remember?"

"José, there are a lot of men named Jesus; there are even more men named García. Which Jesus García are you talking about?"

"Woman, I am talking about *the* Jesus García, the one who saved the entire town of Nacozari in 1907."

"Is he the one who drove the trainload of burning dynamite out of town?"

"Yes, that one. He refused to jump from his locomotive until the train was out of town. Brave man that he was, he waited too long. When the entire train blew up, the locomotive was blown to bits, and Jesus García along with it. They never found even a piece of his body. He saved Nacozari. With an explosion that big, the whole town and everybody in it would have vanished. But Jesus García saved the town. If he had not done what he did, there might not have been a Jimmy Douglas or a Little Daisy Mine here today. Why don't you say a prayer for Jesus García, while I go find Jimmy Douglas? I won't be long."

"Hurry back. I will be worried until I know that he is not going to fire you or kick us off this land because I was not more polite!"

"Don't worry," he said as he left.

José came back two hours later and told Aurelia, "See, I told you it was nothing to worry about. Mr.

Douglas said that he liked the wine that I made for him last year. He just wanted to ask me to make wine again this year. Isn't that great? Of course, I will make a little extra for us."

"I have to tell you, though, that before I left, Mr. Douglas said to me, 'I was watching your wife wash your shirts. She does a fine job. Do you think that she will wash some shirts for me?' Of course I said that you would be glad to do so. He offered to pay for the service, but I told him that it would be an insult to both of us if he would not accept your work as a gesture of our esteem for him."

"José, you were certainly right in refusing any payment. He's been very good to us, so I will be glad to wash his shirts. I think it is quite a compliment. Just bring his shirts to me and I will do an extra good job for him."

When José brought Jimmy Douglas' shirts to Aurelia, she took extra care to make certain that the shirts were clean. She washed them separately and used water that was hotter than usual. The water was hot enough to turn her hands red, but she didn't mind. After she had washed the shirts with care, she hung them out to dry where they would get the most sunshine and the freshest breeze. When the shirts were dry, she took them inside to iron them.

Aurelia set up her ironing board next to her stove, because she needed to heat her iron on the stove top. But when she started to iron the shirts, she noticed that all were missing some buttons, and three of the shirts had small tears. Although the collars were presentable enough, the shirts were obviously well worn.

After she had finished her work, Aurelia was satisfied that she had done a good job. She walked to the Douglas Mansion to deliver in person the freshly pressed and neatly starched shirts to Jimmy Douglas.

He untied the string that held the shirts in a neat stack, and lifted off the first shirt. He looked it over carefully and said, "You have done a fine job. These shirts look great! But you have repaired them, haven't you *señora*?"

"Yes I have. But Mr. Douglas, excuse me for saying it, but I couldn't help wondering about something," she said, with her eyes twinkling and a mischievous smile on her face.

"What were you wondering?"

"I was wondering why a man like you, who is a millionaire, the owner of the mine, who lives in a big mansion, who makes more money in a day than my husband could make in his entire life, why do you wear shirts that need such mending?"

He responded in perfect Spanish, without guile and with complete simplicity, "One is obliged to save for the beans!" (*Hay que guardar para los frijoles!*)

Aurelia tried hard to keep from laughing, but she couldn't contain herself, and her laughter burst out through her pursed lips. She was afraid of Jimmy Douglas' reaction, and she was greatly relieved when he too burst into laughter. Then they laughed together without restraint, until Aurelia stopped to catch her breath.

Finally, she recovered herself enough to say, a little shamefacedly, "With your permission, I had better go home now."

James Douglas said, "Wait a moment, please. Before you go, I want you to promise that you will keep taking care of my shirts for me. But since you won't take any money, I want to give you a present."

He came back with a beautiful serving dish made in France, of very high quality and obviously expensive. It was ivory in color, of fine china, with a circular base of about eight inches in diameter. It flared upwards gracefully to a wider bowl at the top. The rim was gilded with many small squares of pure gold alternating with squares of cobalt blue.

"Here," he said, "It is a present from me. I want to give this to you, not to pay you, but so that you will have a good memory of me. I received this dish many years ago, when Georges Clemenceau, the prime minister of France came to visit me. He brought me a fine set of dishes all the way from France and this serving dish is a part of that set. He and I got along so well, and he bought so much copper from me, that I decided to name a town after him. Do you know the place down in the valley where the smelter for the Little Daisy Mine is located? I decided to name the place Clemenceau in honor of my friend. I could have named the town after me, but doesn't Clemenceau sound a lot better than something like Douglasdale, or Douglasville?"

Aurelia was shocked. "Mr. Douglas, I can't take this present from you. It is much too good for me, and besides, it was a present that a very important man gave to you. Look at me, I'm just a poor simple woman. I don't deserve anything as fine as this!"

"Don't say things like that. You are a fine woman, and I want to honor you. You may do what you want with it; sell it if you want, but I want you to have it. Besides, señora, I know that in Mexico it is considered bad manners to refuse a gift that is offered to you. So here I am offering it to you, and I hope that you do not hurt my feelings by refusing it. Let me wrap it up for you, so that it will not break on your way home."

Aurelia said, "Don't worry, Mr. Douglas, I will always take good care of your gift. I will treasure it for the rest of my life!"

She took home the precious gift and placed it in her cupboard, in the back, where it would not be chipped or scratched. Of course the dish looked completely out of place among her tin cups and mismatched plates, but there it stayed.

Twenty years passed. Many changes took place. Aurelia's husband died of tuberculosis and heartbreak when he realized that he could no longer work. The Little Daisy Mine closed its operations; its rich deposits of copper, silver and gold had been completely exhausted. Jimmy Douglas moved away from his mansion, and Aurelia heard that he had died. In fact, the whole town of Jerome seemed to be dying, looking as if it could never recover.

But Aurelia still lived in the same house by the old cemetery road, where she was living on that day when she first met Jimmy Douglas. From her house she could see the Douglas Mansion, neglected and in disrepair, on the opposite side of the canyon. With no job, no income and no savings, life looked very grim for Aurelia.

Aurelia's sister moved into the house with her, because the sister was also without an income. There was no Social Security, no welfare or assistance of any kind. When their food started to run out, their situation became desperate, and Aurelia realized that unless they could figure out some way to survive, they would both end up dead in their beds, starved to death. She visualized herself dead on her bed, but with the precious dish, which she had come to call *"La Copa,"* beside her.

In a desperate gamble, the two sisters went to Lomeli's meat market in Jerome and bought a pork roast on credit, along with some corn, corn husks and chili powder – all the necessary ingredients for making tamales. After an afternoon of work, they had six dozen tamales ready for sale. They took the hard walk uphill to the business district of Jerome; each woman carrying a bucket of tamales in each hand.

Fortunately, their first stop was at Paul and Jerry's Saloon, where they offered their tamales for sale at 5 cents each. Their venture would have failed right at the beginning, had not Jerry, the proprietor, refused to buy them at that price, because it was obvious to him that the sisters could not make any money by selling the tamales at 5 cents each. He suggested a more sensible price, a price that would make them a profit. They accepted the kind suggestion, and sold all the tamales they were carrying.

After that start, they continued their tamale business, and they supported themselves for decades by making and selling tamales. Few people knew their given names of Aurelia and Santos, but everyone knew them as the "Tamale Ladies." Aurelia and Santos nurtured and helped each other into their old age. Santos died at the age of 103. Aurelia, at one hundred years of age, was still healthy enough to live alone, to prepare meals for herself, and do her own washing. Her eyes could still thread a needle without glasses.

Aurelia was well aware that she would not live forever. Gradually, she started giving away her few material possessions piece by piece. She gave her husband's pistol to the son of a man she knew from the old days, and gave a small gold cross to his wife.

What troubled her most, however, was the question of what to do with her most cherished possession, La Copa, the dish that had been given to her long ago by Jimmy Douglas. She considered donating La Copa to the Town of Jerome, because she wanted "to do something for the Town that has been so good to me." She expected that the Town would be able to auction the dish and use the proceeds for Town purposes. However, she changed her mind when it was suggested to her that a local auction would probably not return the real value of the dish, and might be bought by someone who would not appreciate its historical significance.

One day, as Aurelia stood in her yard and looked across the canyon at Jimmy Douglas' now-restored gleaming white mansion, she thought about that day long ago when she first met him over a boiling tub of wash water and when they later had a good laugh over "saving for the beans." At that moment she knew where La Copa belonged. She would take La Copa home, back to Jimmy's house.

Postscript

Jimmy Douglas' mansion is now the Jerome State Historic Park and Aurelia's La Copa is on display there now, where it will remain forever.

Exodus

"Will you do me a favor? Take me on this trip, but on the back roads, please? I want you to show me more of your beautiful Arizona. I have seen Phoenix and Tucson. They are different, but I have seen plenty of big cities back East. I want to see something that makes your state unique."

The college history professor tucked his thumbs into his belt and in his best John Wayne imitation, said, "Why I'd be right proud to show you, ma'am, you purty little gal. I am going to take you to the most unique town in America, it is called ..."

She interrupted him to say, "David, that's bad grammar! Either a town is unique, or it isn't! There can be no 'most unique!' There are no gradations of uniqueness."

Still doing his imitation, he responded, "That's why I married an Eastern school marm, ma'am. For you to chip away my rough edges."

He agreed to take back roads, so they left Phoenix with the convertible top down on their new car, and headed towards Prescott. The air was cooler in Prescott, and very pleasant driving through the pine trees. The sun warmed the pine sap so that the trees gave off the clean smell of pine woods. After Prescott, the couple headed east to the mountains. They crossed Mingus Summit at 7200 feet, then followed a winding road downhill, to the intended destination of Jerome, Arizona.

A few miles from Jerome, they stopped at an abandoned copper mine that Anne, the professor's wife, wanted to explore.

David stopped the car on a rocky road that led to the mine. They crossed a dry creek bed and came to a locked gate with a faded sign that said, "UV Central," and below that, "No Trespassing." David did not want to trespass, but Anne had already gone past the gate, easing her way through the space between the iron gate and the barbed wire fence.

Ever the professor, David assumed the voice he used in his lectures. "What you are going to see is a mining town that died of old age. Mines go through evolution just like humans. When this mine was a child, its ore body had to be nurtured. As more good ore was found, the mine-child grew into a rowdy boisterous young man, full of strength and vitality. You can tell that this mine was a strong, large operation, judging by the size of the tailings dump."

Anne looked at him and raised her eyebrows.

"The tailings are the waste that had to be removed from the tunnels and shafts before they could get to the good rock, the ore, probably copper in this case. Because the tailings are big, that means that a lot of underground mining took place.

"After that, the mine moved into its middle years, in which the rowdy young mine became more productive. Mining settled into a routine, and more wealth was produced."

"Yes, dear," said Anne, as she walked over to inspect a broken down building. David followed her, still lecturing.

"You can see by the head frame over there that there was a shaft that went down into the earth, who knows how deep it went. On the right you can see some old concrete foundations of homes. Up the hill I can see some remnants of a railroad bed that ran between the shaft and a small smelter built to refine the copper ores. This was a big operation at one time; but then, like people, it got old and wasn't worth much to anybody. That's what you are seeing here. Only the remains of a place that was once very much alive."

"It's sad, isn't it, David?" said Anne, looking around at the ruins of the mine.

"Yes, sad but inevitable. There isn't a single mining town that has ever escaped the same fate. Same as we die, all mining towns die."

"Oh, David, let's not talk about death and dying."

"Well, we still have another old mining town ahead of us, and I am not sure what we will find, so I wanted to prepare you. But Jerome is quite a place. Let's go on."

The road to Jerome had been blasted through some of the hardest and oldest rocks on earth. The mountainsides were very steep, so a level surface for the road had to be blasted foot by foot. Because it took so much effort to build it, the road was only a two-lane narrow road. The deep gorge and hairpin turns scared off many drivers.

"Please drive carefully, David. It's a long way down and I see nothing but jagged rocks at the bottom." Anne seemed fascinated as well as scared, and she remained absorbed, with her gaze fixed on the bottom of the canyon. When she raised her eyes to look straight ahead, she raised her right hand to her mouth to stifle a gasp. She saw nothing but blue sky straight ahead!

"Oh, my God! What happened to the road? Stop the car, David!"

"Don't worry, the road's still there," said David as he slowed down. "Have you ever seen a more dramatic entrance to a town?" he asked as he turned onto a narrow pull-out.

"It is magnificent! I'm sure I'll appreciate it more once I get over being scared to death."

They got out of the car and walked to the guard rail. The road turned left, but straight ahead the mountain dropped in an almost vertical drop to the town, far below. They could see houses that looked a fraction of their real size. Anne braced herself against the guard rail to prevent vertigo.

After they admired the view, David pointed to a road sign that said, "You Are Entering Jerome, The Most Unique Town in America."

"See," he said, "Do you know of any other town in America where you can be at an elevation of 3500 feet at the lower end of town, but at over 5000 feet above sea level at the upper end? It is a unique town, even if it did get its grammar wrong. Come on."

As they entered the town, they passed houses that needed paint, whose woodwork was rotted and broken. They passed a three-story cement building that looked like an abandoned apartment building. The windows were broken, and many tiles were missing from the roof. On the other side of the road was another large concrete building with a faded sign that said, "T. F. Miller Company."

The road passed another empty building with Spanish arches, and now they were driving on what appeared to be the main street of Jerome. However, none of the businesses were open. Some stores had windows that were boarded up; others had windows with the broken glass still hanging.

There were no people anywhere to be seen, except two old women who were walking towards them. They were wearing identical brown dresses that reached halfway to their ankles, and had black shawls over their heads. They were each carrying a metal bucket. They walked slowly and purposefully and passed their car without a word or a glance at them.

Anne said, "I feel like I am in a time warp or the twilight zone! What is going on here?" She looked around and said, "Where are all the people?"

When she looked to her left, she saw a man wearing a white apron, about a block away on a side street. She pointed the man out to her husband, who turned into the side street and parked in front of a small restaurant whose sign said "English Kitchen."

The man in the white apron stood in front of the business. He was an older Chinese man, who waited until the couple got out of the car, wiped his hands on his apron, and went inside to stand behind a counter. In front of the counter were ten stools with round wooden tops that rotated on metal pedestals. The opposite wall had a row of five booths painted a dull green; wooden partitions separated each booth. Near the door, two menus tacked on the wall advertised a three-course meal for 25 cents, including coffee. The menus were dated 1945, twenty-two years ago.

The couple walked into the restaurant, and David asked, "Do you serve breakfast?"

"Bleakfast? You betcha!" the man answered with a thick Chinese accent.

"What do you have?"

"Chicken flied steak, flied both sides."

"Anything else?"

"Chicken flied steak, flied both sides."

David declined, and said, "Two coffees, please."

One sip of the coffee was all they could take. It tasted like it must have been brewed in 1945.

Anne asked, "What has happened here? Where are all the people?"

The man replied, "Too much too long, not too many customers."

They gave up their quest for information and food, so they thanked the man, and put a dollar bill on the table, and walked out the door.

As they reached their car, another car came around the corner. It was driven by an old man with stiff grey hair on his head, a two-day old growth of hair on his face, and a very large mole on his right chin. But the car was remarkable.

The car had open wheels because the fenders had been taken off. The cab had either been a roadster, or had been converted into one by chopping off the body down to the top of the doors. The back end of the car ended in a boat tail. It looked like a home-made version of a 1903 racing car.

Anne said, "Look at that car! We really are in a time warp – or on another planet. Obviously this was once quite a town. Look at all the big empty buildings! But where have all the normal people gone? I'm beginning to think that you're right about Jerome being, as you say, the 'Most Unique Town in America!' This is fascinating! Can we do a little more exploring?"

They drove from the English Kitchen into what was obviously a residential area, but must have been a very poor one, even in its prime. The houses were cheaply constructed with narrow battens that had once covered the cracks in between the boards. The lumber had warped and discolored, and every board had cracks from top to bottom.

The houses all leaned downhill, and some also leaned sideways, as if a leg had been knocked out from under them. The houses in the worst condition were the ones built on the steepest slopes, because while the front of the house was on a level with the road, the back of the house was two or three stories above the lower ground. The only support for these houses were pieces of lumber that were already bowed by the weight and looked to break at any moment. Some houses had already collapsed.

A few houses looked safe enough to enter, so Anne entered one of them: a decrepit house, on a decrepit street, whose decrepit front door was wide open.

"Look at this! Here is the old miner's living room, and there is the old miner's couch!" She pointed at a couch whose cushions had been torn apart by rodents. Along a side wall, there was an old console radio whose veneer had peeled off and fallen to the floor. The linoleum floors of the shack were covered with a film of dust disturbed only by rodent tracks.

"They must have frozen here in the winter," she thought. There was no source of heat except the stove. On the walls, the cracks between the boards were wide enough that she could see the sky. The only insulation on the walls and ceiling was a thin oilcloth. The oilcloth on the ceiling had sagged with the weight of the water that had leaked through the roof.

She called out again, "Honey, look! Here's the old miner's kitchen!"

Silently, she looked at the small wooden table with four chairs scattered about. A broken old hurricane lamp was still on the table, along with a few cups and saucers. One of the cups still smelled of coffee. She opened the cupboard doors, and saw shelves containing bowls, cups, and plates that were a mish-mash of different sets. An aluminum pot was on the stove, still coated with some long-dried substance on the bottom.

A bottle on the counter top looked like a quart beer bottle. She opened a drawer filled with cheap flatware. There was no indoor plumbing that she could see, except for a faucet in the kitchen sink.

She walked carefully into one of the bedrooms. The wooden floor creaked with each step, even though she was a very small woman. In the first bedroom she saw a brass bed still made up with sheets, blankets and pillows. Men's and women's clothing still hung in the closet. In another bedroom, she saw two twin beds without mattresses.

She blurted to David who walked up beside her, "Everything is still here! It's eerie!"

David said, "This reminds me of Pompeii, where people were buried in their houses by volcanic ash. But at least in Pompeii, the people were still there. Here there is no one. This reminds me more of the exodus of the Sinagua Indians from this valley. They just left their dwellings intact and moved away. Nobody knows for certain why it happened."

While the man was talking, the woman realized that she was looking at the remains of someone's life. A life, or lives, that she knew nothing about. Obviously, though, this life had ended abruptly, otherwise all these things would not have been left behind. She felt a great sadness come over her, and began to feel like an intruder who had entered into someone's home uninvited.

She said, "David, I don't want to be here anymore. I feel that I am disturbing the dreams of the people who once lived here, and I feel very sad for them. Please, let's get out of here and go on to Flagstaff." She went out the door without closing it, not waiting for a reply.

———

The quarrels of the Lopez family had been going on for several months. The subject of the quarrels was always the same: the wife wanted to leave Jerome, but the husband wanted to stay. Subsets of the quarrel were the husband's frequent drinking, and the wife's fear of her husband's dangerous work in the mine. Their quarrel always reached a crescendo on payday, then quieted down in between, but always it peaked again on the following payday.

On this payday, the third Friday in August of 1947, the husband, Achilles Lopez, arrived home from work about 7:30 pm, two and a half hours later than usual.

His wife, Leonor, recognized the sound of the engine of his Model A Ford truck, and knew that he was driving a little too fast. Achilles braked a little harder than normal, so the tires slid on the gravel surface before the truck came to a complete stop. Leonor heard the clink of bottles as they rolled forward from under the seat of the truck.

"*Viejo*, you've been drinking again, haven't you?" She called him "old man" as a term of familiar endearment, but he was only thirty years old.

"Only two beers, *Vieja*," he answered with a charming smile. He called her "old lady," though she was only twenty-seven years old, and only ten years older than when she was the Beauty Queen of the Jerome Mexican Independence Day celebration.

"You must not have been very thirsty, if you only drank two beers in all that time," she said.

"I was talking with the men uptown."

It was true, he had in fact been talking with men, other miners who gathered at Paul and Jerry's Saloon after every shift. On paydays, the bar was even more crowded, with miners lined up eight deep in front of the bar. The noise level was high with all the conversations going on at the same time. The common thread of conversations was work in the mine.

"I finished drilling by 2:30 today." "Two more beers, please." "That damn rock almost fell on me." "I blasted a little after three." "I've never seen such damn hard rock." "The new guy didn't even last a day, he couldn't take it." "It was hotter than hell at the 4300-level." "My foreman doesn't know a damn thing about mining." "Let me buy you a beer." "Here's the money I owe you." "Did you hear about the accident on the night shift?" "That damn chute got away from me and I had to climb up the man-way fast as I could!" "The Tiger Mine, now there was a mine. It had copper, gold, silver, moly, everything." "Bisbee was never like this!"

The men shared the camaraderie of men who had been through something dangerous but had survived. They drew strength from being around a group of other men who shared the same experiences. It was strength they needed to go to their dark, dangerous work the next day, and the day after that. It was something that Achilles' wife could not understand.

After being with the men in the bar, Achilles could turn his attention to the wife and family whom he loved very much. His wife was still lovely to look at, even though she had borne him one daughter and three sons in their ten years of marriage. She had light brown hair and green eyes and had kept her delicate frame that had made her a beauty. His arms closed around her and she said, "When are you going to quit the mine, as you have promised me, about a million times? Did you give them notice today?"

"Don't start that again, Vieja."

"I'm never going to stop, Viejo. Because you don't know what it is like, staying home alone with four children, not knowing whether you are alive or dead inside that mine. It's not until I hear your truck coming that I can feel myself relax. Did you give your notice today that you were quitting, or didn't you?"

"I couldn't do it. We don't have any money saved up, and I have no time to find another job, even if there were other places where I could find man's work. I don't want to be a clerk in a grocery store, even if we could live on those earnings. You know we can't."

"Viejo, we've been going over these same arguments for months now. We have never been able to settle anything, and I have given up hope in believing that you will ever be able to quit. I don't want to go on arguing about this forever. You know that I argue with you only because I truly love you, don't you?"

"You've told me that before, and I believe you, honey."

"It's getting harder and harder for me to bear. We all know that the mine is closing down. I don't want my husband to be one of the last men to be killed in a mine, just as I would not want my son to be killed on the last day of the war."

The husband said, "You have told me that before, Vieja. Next, you are going to tell me that 'you don't know what you would do as a widow trying to raise four small children by yourself.'"

She stiffened into a posture of determination, and raised her voice to say,"Well that settles it. We have gone over these same things so much that we both know what the other is going to say. We just go over the same things all the time. There is no use to argue anymore, so we will have no more arguments tonight. Your brother Mike brought us a nice present, this big sirloin steak. We are going to have that, and some squash with cheese that you like so much. And just to show you that I'm not going to argue with you anymore about your drinking, I have two quart bottles of Acme beer cold and ready for you. Now give me a kiss, Viejo!" She put her arms around him.

Achilles enjoyed his meal, and the beer. Immediately afterwards, he fell asleep on the couch, as his wife knew that he would. Then she started to put her plan into effect. First, she loaded the children's mattresses and two pillows into the floor of the truck bed, and told the children that they could sleep outside in the truck. Of course they loved the idea. After they had fallen asleep, she put some bags of food and some drinking water in the truck. She left the passenger door of the truck open, and went back inside the house to get her husband. "Come on Viejo, it's time to go to bed." He got up with her help, half asleep, but instead of leading him to their bedroom, she led him outside the house and into the passenger seat of the truck. She cushioned his head against a pillow and closed the door. Finally, she went back into the house for a last look. She went first into their bedroom, and saw the bedcovers turned down for the night. She recalled that the covers had been turned down the same way when they had moved into this house on their wedding night. She turned off the light as the first tear fell across her cheek. Then she went into the children's bedroom where her children had slept since they were born. The tears were flowing freely now. She first turned off the bedroom light, then the light in the kitchen, and finally the living room light. She whispered a silent goodbye to the silent house, then she closed the door slowly and sadly, with fear as well as determination. She turned her back to the house, and went to the truck, on the driver's side. She had never driven a car by herself before, ever.

As the sun rose above the horizon and her red, sleepy eyes scratched painfully each time she blinked, Leonor reached over and shook her husband.

"Viejo, wake up. You have to drive now." He roused himself, befuddled, and was even more bewildered as he realized that he had not been sleeping in his own bed.

"Where are we?" he asked.

"Near Ash Fork."

"How in hell did we get here? What are we doing here?" he asked as he looked out the side window at the unfamiliar flat land.

"We are on our way to California."

"We are?"

"Yes, we are," she said very firmly. "And I need you to drive now. I'm too tired and can't drive anymore."

Achilles knew that their argument was over. He did not even ask her how she had managed to drive over the mountain in the dark. Instead, he got behind the steering wheel and they continued on the road to California. Their old life in Jerome was behind them. Their new life was somewhere down the road ahead.

About the Author

Roberto Rabago was born in Jerome and grew up in the house depicted on the front cover of this book. He moved to California and graduated from Fresno State University, University of Santa Clara Law School, and University of California Law School. He now lives in Jerome, Arizona.